Will Hubbard- Kernan, John R Clymer

The Flaming Meteor

Will Hubbard- Kernan, John R Clymer

The Flaming Meteor

ISBN/EAN: 9783337327965

Printed in Europe, USA, Canada, Australia, Japan

Cover: Foto ©Andreas Hilbeck / pixelio.de

More available books at **www.hansebooks.com**

THE FLAMING METEOR

POETICAL WORKS

OF

WILL HUBBARD-KERNAN

BIOGRAPHY BY

HON. JOHN R. CLYMER

OF OHIO

CHICAGO
CHARLES H. KERR AND COMPANY
175 DEARBORN STREET
1892

CONTENTS

Contents

4

Contents 5

PREFACE

In presenting the present volume to the public, I realize that it is a risky venture, for the
literary market has long been surfeited with
verse, and the impression has gone forth that
the "poets are all dead."

A certain nineteenth-century censor once
said: "All poetry was written by men who were
dead and dust before any of us were born;
and it is impossible to conceive an idea of a
poetical type younger than the bards who
went down to death before America had been
awaked to civilization." But I hold that the
censor in question was too sweeping in his
assertion; that, in the advance of time, new
thoughts, feelings and ambitions have come to
animate humanity; that lofty and luminous sentiments have sprung from the laws of liberty,
unknown in the time when the Blind Bard of
Scio swept his harp; that all best and brightest
literature is the consummate flower of the cycle
that is now thundering and throbbing into the
eternity which it will forever electrify.

In introducing to the world in book form
the poetical works of Will Hubbard-Kernan,
I feel that I am rescuing from the "rounds of
the press" some of the choicest flowers that
bedeck American literature, which will raise
from obscurity and darkness, into the blazing
light of a never-ending day, a name that shall
endure among the great of our country.

Whatever difference of opinion may exist at

present regarding Will Hubbard-Kernan, as a poet, there can be no doubt that he possesses a positive individuality, a certain vein of originality, unapproached by any other living writer, a style and philosophy distinctively his own, and a certain daring forcefulness that defies all preconceived opinions formulated by the church, society and the state.

As a man Kernan stands apart, because few can understand him. He is an intense, I might say vindictive, hater of shams, and he never conceals his opinions or hesitates to speak his creed in unmistakable Saxon. He is a free-thinker in religion and a free-lance in society. His mind is constantly at war with existing conditions. At one time a potent force in politics, he has surrendered and renounced all allegiance to "the powers that be," believing all present forms of government to be radically wrong in vital matters. He is opposed to matrimony and the perpetuation of the species, holding with Schopenhauer that the world is a gigantic swindle, life a dark and dreary tragedy, and that it is a greater crime to bring a soul into this vale of tears than it is to send one out of it.

His poems were written without any other object than to give concrete form to the longings of his own soul, and they combine all the rhythm, melody and motion of an ideal love-song and the volcanic force of a nature that sees all, feels all and fears nothing.

While we may not admit the prevailing trend of his philosophy, which has a decided tendency toward pessimism, and is in conflict with accepted ideas in many instances, still there is in his songs an inexplicable tenderness

and pathos that appeal to every heart, a
magnetism that enchains every mind, and we
are impelled irresistibly to bow in admiration
to the force and energy of his intellect. He
seems to have swept with a master's hand over
the whole scale of human feeling—to have
sounded in turn each of life's notes, except
that bright, joyous one, in which the lesser
poets so delight to revel.

*   *   *   *   *

Readers of this volume will readily discern
that Mr. Kernan's life at times has been darkened by heavy shadows. Every line of his
sad, sweet verses, perhaps unknown to himself, betrays the "anguish of the singer." In
his famous "Song of Hate," a bitter arraign-
ment of the world of sham and sin, he most
forcibly presents his estimate of life and the
pleasure he finds in his share in it:—

> For since the first, fierce morning of time with its toils and
> tears,
> Down through the dim, long vista of fleet and fugitive years,
> I see but the one black picture, 'twixt cradle and coffin-bed,
> Of conquering knaves
> And cowering slaves,
> And the doom that struck them dead.

The general gloom that casts its melancholy
shadow over his soul is but the reflection of
his sad and stormful career. Born at a time
when the dissentient sections of our common ·
country were preparing to march into the tears,
blood and agony of civil war, his youth was
embittered by the hates, crimes and passions of
that tumultuous epoch. Unfortunately for him,
Kernan's early sympathies went out to the
people of the South, and he championed their
cause with all the force and ardor of his soul.

As editor of the Okolona (Miss.) *States*, he spoke his sentiments in "language as hot and hissing as a musket-ball on the wing"—I quote his own words—and for his impolitic utterances of Southern opinion he was subjected to the most bitter partisan denunciation. Prompted by artful machinators, the Northern press, of his own party, joined in the clamor, branding him a "Republican in disguise," and a spy who had been sent into the South for the purpose of kindling anew the flames of civil strife. This infamous libel served well the purpose of his treacherous traducers. The more ignorant masses of the old Confederacy became incensed against him; insidious enemies in both sections sprang forward to vent their latent spite, and the courage of his friends, with a few noble and notable exceptions, gave way before the godless crusade.

For years Kernan has been the victim of political persecutions, and a pitiless fate has dogged his path with such unrelenting malevolence, that the naturally morose and melancholy tendency of his mind has been greatly intensified.

*   *   *   *   *

If Mr. Kernan is of a pessimistic trend of mind, it is owing to the foregoing facts; and the thinking, discerning, unprejudiced reader will remember them in making up his judgment on the unorthodox sentiments of his poetry.

Consider why the change was wrought,
You'll find it his misfortune, not his fault.

R. D. KATHRENS.

WILL HUBBARD-KERNAN

A SKETCH OF HIS LIFE, AND HIS CHARACTERISTICS
AS A JOURNALIST AND A POET

The people of Verona, when they saw Dante on the streets, used to say, "*Eccovi l'uom ch'i stato all'Inferno!*"—("See, there is the man that was in hell!") Ah, yes, he had been in hell—in hell enough, in long sorrows and struggle, as the like of him is pretty sure to have been. . . Perhaps one would say, intensity, with the much that depends on it, is the prevailing character of Dante's genius; partly the fruit of his position, but partly of his own nature. His greatness has, in all senses, concentered itself into fiery emphasis and depths. . . There is a brevity, an abrupt precision, in him. Tacitus is not briefer, more condensed; and then in Dante it seems a natural condensation, spontaneous to the man. One smiting word, and there is darkness. Strange with what a sharp, decisive grace he snatches the true likeness of a matter: cuts into it as with a pen of fire.—[*Thomas Carlyle.*

Will Hubbard-Kernan, the subject of my sketch, first saw the light in the beautiful and historic Mac-o-chee Valley, Ohio. His father, the late Judge Kernan (lineally descended from the celebrated Kernans of the Emerald Isle), an eloquent and successful lawyer, removed with his wife, a lady of beauty and brilliant talents, to Bellefontaine, Ohio, in 1848, where he resided until his death, in July, 1883, enjoying the honors and fruits of active, professional life. Wm. Hubbard, one of the most brilliant poets and powerful journalists of the great West, and Thomas Hubbard, one of the ablest and most humorous of our political writers—uncles on the mother's side—are among the many of his family whose gifts and achievements impelled him to tread the thorny as well as the flowery paths of intellectual endeavor and fame. He attended the Academy at Bellefontaine several years. In 1866 he attended the University at

Ann Arbor, Mich., graduating in the law-class in 1868. Returning home, he wrote for the press until 1870, winning favorable commendations from the Fourth Estate.

Attracted by his sentiments, and nervous, energetic style of writing, Mr. Kernan was invited by Hon. Wm. M. Corry to Cincinnati, Ohio, who associated him with the editorial department of the "Commoner," where he exhibited remarkable power as a political writer.

Resigning his position, he became a reporter for the News Association in New York City. After a short service in the metropolis he was appointed editor-in-chief of the Ft. Wayne, Ind., daily "Sentinel"—one of the leading Democratic organs of the West—doing signal service for his party. He resigned to assume an editorship on the Indianapolis "Sentinel." His radical utterances created a host of enemies among the vacillating Democracy, and seeing himself abused, maligned, unappreciated, in the house of his friends in the North, he went South in 1875, and the next year became editor of the Okolona "States," of Mississippi. That prodigy of Southern journalism, under the magical utterances of his pen, displayed a boldness and an intensity of expression perhaps never equaled, certainly never excelled, by any American paper. It was the subject of grave discussion in Congress, as well as in leading magazines, and its scathing, catapult editorials were copied and commented on by the press of all parties throughout the land. No such flaming meteor ever blazed across the political heavens. Many, both North and South, disputed the correctness of its principles and conclusions; but all, even its fiercest enemies, admitted its earnestness and ability. In a short period this hitherto obscure village journal ran up to more than ten thousand circulation. An unfortunate difference between editor and proprietor (the latter having placed the former in a false position on certain political matters) caused Mr. Kernan's resignation, and instantly the Okolona meteor was extinguished. As La Crosse was, is now, and for long will be known as the place where Brick Pomeroy published his "Democrat," so Okolona is known abroad, like a household word, for the only reason that Will H. Kernan there, for a few brief years, shot out from its obscurity the blazing light of his fiery genius.

In the summer of 1880 he assumed the position of staff-correspondent of the Chicago "Tribune," still writing in his usual Democratic vein. In connection with a friend he started the career of the "Solid South" at Memphis, Tenn., December, 1880. Retiring from that enterprise, he went up into the Cumberland Mountains, seeking health and pleasure, where he wrote for several political and literary journals of prominence. At the same time he began writing those remarkable poems that appeared in "Meriwether's Weekly," the leading literary paper of the South, under the *nom de plume* of "Kenneth Lamar." But concerning his poetry let me not anticipate.

In 1881 he went North and became identified with Iowa journalism. While editing the Odebolt "Observer" in that State he was selected as a delegate to a Democratic convention, whereupon certain unprincipled schemers in his party formed a conspiracy to keep him out of that body because of his Okolona record.

The plot was successful, and disgusted with his treatment, Mr. Kernan withdrew from politics to become the editor of an independent paper at Orange City, Iowa. Since then he has been identified at different times with the press of Arkansas, North Dakota, Kansas, New York, Michigan and Minnesota, and his strange, stormful career in the field of journalism would make a volume of more intense interest than any novel of our century.

*   *   *

Personally, Mr. Kernan has gray eyes, black hair, stands five feet, eleven and a-half inches in his shoes, weighs 160 pounds, is straight as an Indian, what ladies would call handsome, and possesses a fine intellectual head and expressive countenance. But no one would suspect for a moment that he was the whilom "fire-eater" of the "Okolona States" or "Solid South." As mild a mannered man as ever danced attendance to my "ladye fayre," he is the most fierce, scathing, sarcastic, political writer—the most terrible master of invective since Junius made the King of England tremble on his throne. His vocabulary of words is wonderful, and yet no person can, or ever does, mistake his meaning. His short, crisp, staccato style was invented by him, and he uses it for the double purpose of giving his thoughts piquancy and exclamatory force. Woe to the upstarts who provoke his wrath, for he not only demolishes, but annihilates. Had he lived in the Middle Ages, when chivalry was in its glory, he would have been one of the truest and bravest knights that ever shivered lance or flashed sword in vindication of woman's virtue, the Cross of Christ or the Holy Sepulcher.

Intensity of feeling and vehement expression characterize each of his productions. Never made to be a slave, the poet's aspiration is his own:

"Thy spirit, Independence, let me share—
Lord of the lion-heart and eagle-eye!
Thy steps I follow with my bosom bare,
Nor heed the storm that howls along the sky."

A brilliant meteor in journalism, he fills a void, hitherto unattempted, no other can fill. Agreeable to taste, conviction or prejudice, critics will differ as to his merits in this respect, but all will admit his fierce candor, clear-cut style and unmistakable originality. A Democrat of the Jefferson and Calhoun type, he is independent, incisive, too little accustomed to

"——crook the pregnant hinges of the knee,
That thrift may follow fawning,"

to ever become in the popular sense a great political leader. Of orthodox religious parentage, yet he is predisposed to Agnosticism—not from natural instinct or inner consciousness, but rather as the result of an Ishmael life in journalism and a fierce contest with the elemental forces of politics, causing his hand to be against every man and every man's hand against him. Truly it can be said of him as it was said of Dante: "There is the man that was in hell!"

So much of Mr. Kernan, his birth, personnel, life-pursuits and principles, all with special reference to a correct interpretation of him in his more pleasing and exalted character of poet—for be it known unto you, O most wise critics, North and South, that he is one of the truest and worthiest that ever swept his hands across the strings of our country's lyre.

Poetry is the gift of God—his voice speaking through man to men. Not college-bred nor self-made, the genuine poet is he who feels, speaks, sings or writes the inspiraitons of the High and Holy One who inhabiteth Eternity. That inspiration is an inexplicable mystery. Like the wind, it bloweth where it listeth; thou hearest the sound thereof but canst not tell whence it cometh or whither it goeth.

Vapor, generated in the bosom of our planet, escapes, ascending through its earthquake-riven shell to the surface of the Arkansian Hot Springs, condenses in pure, limpid, healing waters, differing in temperature, quality and magnetism. So these inspirations of the Supreme, that men call poetry, differ in the same ratio, according to the physical, mental and moral organisms through which they come to bless or curse mankind.

.At proper times God said: "Let there be light—let Homer, Virgil, Dante, Shakespeare and Milton be." And it was so. They came, and brought with them the Iliad, Æneid, Inferno, Hamlet and Paradise Lost. He looked on them and pronounced them "good."

These, and all other poets, came because they were wanted. Predestined to sing their immortal verses and utter the prophetic verities, necessary to be uttered at various and proper times, they were "the called, according to his purpose."

There were fewer major than minor prophets in the olden times, but all were divinely sent, and each had a specific mission. And so with poets, for each had his time, place and purpose. It is not for the creature to say to its creator, "Why am I thus?"

Our nineteenth century has had no major poet sent to it. From Byron, Tennyson, Longfellow, and Edgar A. Poe. to Walt Whitman, they are all minors. Yet God be thanked for them, every one! They fulfill their mission and destiny:

Without further prelude, let me introduce the poet Kernan, to you, O gentle reader! and, presenting some of his verses—mere *disjecta membra* of his poems—ask the suffrage of your kind and considerate judgment. For the sake of convenience and perspicuity, his poems may be divided into descriptive, patriotic and Agnostic.

In 1868, he gave to the public, in the Bucyrus (O.) *Forum*, "The Dream of a Dream," which at the time was approved by competent judges as possessing uncommon merit. The reader will observe the power of description. exhibited in his youth, in the following stanzas culled from it at random:

I live with old memorial things—I wander spaces wide.

     *   *   .*   *

Hot Afric jungles, thick and green, before my vision rise
A cruel tiger crouches there with bright and burning eyes,
And in the shadow of a palm a naked native stands,
With lifted spear—the savage son of still more savage lands.
I see the desert stretching dim before mine aching eyes,
Oases with their plumy palms carved green against the skies,
And black Assyrian ruins where the tents of Arabs gleam,
And the solemn site of Tyre, where the fisher dreams his
    dream.

If Bryant or Longfellow had written that line,

Oases with their plumy palms carved green against the skies,

how the critics of Boston would have shouted themselves hoarse in its praise!

"Found" is full of splendid word-painting, and is a fair specimen of Kernan's descriptive power. Read this:

> ...... The foamy waves
> Were chiming at my feet a tune
> That sounded like the subtle rune
> Of some lost paradisic staves,
> When, suddenly, before my sight
> Stood up a city, vast and white,
> With strange, majestic temple-walls, .
> Deserted streets and voiceless halls,
> With dumb, proud idols, ruined shrines,
> Urns stained with sacrificial wines.

> *   *   *   *   *

> And thus the lost was found, and thus
> From uttermost of continents,
> We were led back to love intense,
> By ways that were unknown to us—
> By ways we never would have trod,
> Save through the guidance of a god.

What a grandly poetical description is this, from Kernan's celebrated poem, "Southland," read at the thirteenth Annual Convention of the Mississippi Press Association, at Vicksburg, June, 1878:

O, Southland, loveliest land beneath the bright blue-bending skies!
O, land most passionate this side the gates of Paradise!
A sense of gladness unconfined was mine when first I set
My foot upon thy flowery sod; it lingers with me yet.
I love thy immemorial hills by humankind untrod,
The rose-lights of their raptured heights touched by the kiss of God;
The crash and wirble jubilant of cataracts that leap,
And flash, and shimmer through the vines that trail from steep to steep.
I love thy valley-lands; they hold a beauty never sung,
As sweet, as pure, as undefiled as when the world was young;
As then the ripe, wild roses trail their scarlet mists of bloom,
And sparkle sun-lit lily-bells with amber hearts illume;
As then the rivers roll and surge—proud, passionate and free,

Through sweeps of glad savannah-lands, to kiss the golden
    sea.
I love thy wild and waving woods where in the glooms of
    green
The miracle magnolia flowers like fallen moons are seen,
Where mock-birds twitter, pipe and trill through long, re-
    splendent days,
Till leaf and flower seem to dance in rhythm with their lays.

These lines discover the poet's inward wish.
Though born and bred in Ohio he is, and from
childhood has been, a devoted lover of the
Sunny South—whose sympathies are with her
people, politics and institutions. No son of
hers was ever more loyal than he. Occasion-
ally he was moved by this spirit, and verses
of wonderful power were the result. In a
poem of difficult meter, entitled "Our Cause,"
are the following suggestive stanzas:

Go thou to their burial places
  When the crimson and creamy blooms
    Are thridding the greenest grasses,
    Are twining the dim old stones,
And think of their proud, still faces
  In the depths of the desolate tombs,
    And say over them thy masses,
    And vent over them thy moans;
And swear by the blood of thy brothers
  Who fell on the battle-plain—
    Swear by their graves all glorious,
    By the prayers thy sisters prayed,
Swear by the tears of thy mothers,
  By our passion and our pain,
    Forever, until victorious,
    For our Cause to stand arrayed.

"A Song of the Twentieth Century" reads like
some of Tennyson's patriotic verses. It stirs
the soul like a trumpet-blast:

Hosanna! Lift up the bright palm-branches higher,
O, race that was ransomed through flood and through fire!
Ring, stormily ring, O, ye bells in the steeples!

Flash, merrily flash, O, ye flags of the peoples!
The monarchs have fallen—the people are free!
Vive Liberty!

"The Progress of the Peoples" is one of the noblest utterances of the aspirations and eventual elevation of humanity ever made, and certainly the noblest in behalf of woman. This is seen in every detached stanza:

Upward, upward, press the people to that pure exalted plane,
Where no throne shall cast a shadow and no slave shall wear
 a chain.
They have trampled on the fagots, broken crucifix and wheel,
Banished block and thong and hemlock and the headsman's
 bloody steel;
Forced the Church-hold to surrender stake and scourge and
 bolt and bar—
Torn the keys from off its girdle, thrown the Gates of Truth
 ajar.
They have forced the titled tyrants human rights to recognize,
And with bayonet and saber they have slain a legion lies.
They are lighting lamps of freedom on a million altar-stones
With the torches they have kindled at the blaze of burning
 thrones.
  * * * * *
She hath wept and prayed in passion—bitterly hath made her
 moan—
All the terrors and the tortures of the tyrants she hath known;
Still, the blood that flows for Freedom, flows for man, and
 man alone.
She hath borne with man his crosses, she hath worn with man
 his chains,
She hath suffered all his losses, she hath suffered all his pains,
She shall stand with him, co-equal, on the pure, exalted plains!

It is to be regretted that Kernan's mind has latterly become entangled in the fantasies and sophistries of Agnosticism. A universe without a God, a human soul without a future existence, is at once illogical in principle and repugnant to man's highest and holiest aspirations. Some of his most powerful and noticeable verse has been sung in this key. "What

is the Use?" which has been widely published,
answered, and discussed in the public prints,
shows the groping of the poet's soul in the
dark:

> They prate of a phantom world afar,
> Beyond the mold and the marble urn,
> Beyond the fire of the furthest star,
> Where life is immortal and love eterne.
>
> But I am no dupe of their priestly dreams,
> They know of nothing that is to be:
> The light that out of their heaven streams,
> Is the self-same light that shines on me.
>
>   * * * * *
>
> What is the use of it all, I say?
> Why are we brought from the blank Unknown,
> To weep and dance through a little day,
> That drifts us under a burial-stone?

And the following in the same strain:

> O! Fate is cruel, and Fate is cold,
> And only giveth a grave at last;
> And what is glory, or love, or gold,
> When this brief hour is overpast?
>
> What doth it matter us how we live?
> What doth it matter us how we die?
> What can all of the future give
> When under the grassy clods we lie?
>
> What will it matter to you and me—
> Insensate there in immortal calm—
> Whether our funeral dirge shall be
> A reptile's hiss or a nation's psalm?
>
> Whether our friends were false or true,
> Whether our foes were strong or weak,
> What will it matter to me or you,
> After our candle is out? O, speak!

From such cheerless philosophy as this, I
gladly turn to the following outburst of poetic
fervor, in his "Poet-Boy of Mississippi: "

> But there is a Revelation, and it redes itself to man—
> Known it was in every cycle, unto every creed and clan,

Taught the simple heart primeval by the still, small voice
within,
Prompting it to deeds of duty—urging it to shrink from sin,
Pictured on the cliffs and lowlands, chiming in the surge of
seas,
Glowing in the star-dust golden, blossoming in shrubs and
trees,
Beaming in the looks love-lighted of the tender and the true,
Whispered by the lips of spirits sheltered from our mortal
view,
Speaking in our hopes and yearnings, and our dim dreams of
the night,
Tempering our tears and passion when a twin-soul takes its
flight,
Proving stronger and supremer as the world heaves high and .
higher
From the depths of Superstition and the mists of low Desire!
And this Revelation redeth that our Dead have never died—
That it was the yoke and fetters only that they laid aside;
That they live in Kingdom fairer than is lit by mortal sun,
Thrilled with triumph at the conquest and the crown forever
won—
Live where purer joys and purer draw them to diviner plains,
And forever reaching toward them some new happiness re-
mains,
Where with victor-songs of gladness they will welcome us at
last,
When the fitful frost and fever of our lives are overpast.

What a gratifying and refreshing contrast is
this strong language of heart and soul to the
weak jingles of some of our latter-day poets,
who "creep and grovel on the ground" and
never soar above the dew-wet grass and the
beautiful snow!

*   *   *   *

After Edgar Allen Poe, the most brilliant
poetic genius this country has produced, comes
Will Hubbard-Kernan. It is only by reason
of his pronounced Southern principles that
he has been ignored by the *literati* of Boston
and New York; but, fortunately, time and
justice

"At last make all things even."

POEMS OF PESSIMISM

THE CRY OF A CYNIC

Had I known the world as I know it now
  In my boyhood I half believe that I
Would have sworn me a stern, fierce, terri-
    ble vow
  Down unto my death to live a lie;

To promise, yet never perform; to pose
  As a friend, while betraying all friendships
    here;
To prate religion, while under the rose
  I struck through its quivering breast a
    spear.

For I often think had I lived this lie,
  And lived it like many a man I see,
That wealth or power or honor high
  As it came to them would have come to
    me;

Nor would I have felt as I feel to-day,
  When I find how fickle is friendship here;
For, ah! had I been but as false as they,
  I could answer a-back with a sneer for
    sneer;

But—fool that I was!—I trusted so,
  And my love was leal as love could be,
Ah! there is the bitterness of the blow
  That has smitten the·innermost soul of me.

And as for the world that has hissed me
    down
  Unto depths I never had thought to know—

I turn away from its fleer and frown
　Despairing, for it hath deceived me so.

Fool! fool that I was! in my trustful youth
　I thought this world was a world sublime
That was struggling ever in search of Truth,
　And where Truth would triumph in time—
　　in time;

And I tried to teach it the Right as I
　Could see the Right, in my own weak way,
And it sprang upon me with curse and cry
　And is hounding me down like a dog to-day.

But far between, and though few they be,
　Are good, grand souls in this world of
　　shame,
And the love and lilies they send to me
　Are more than fortune and more than fame;

And when I remember these royal men
　I rise renewed in my sense and soul,
And take up the trials of life again,
　And again press on to a golden goal.

IN THE JUNGLE

Tiger, tiger! in thy lair,
　Thou hast torn his limbs apart;
O, the white bones lying there!
　O, the red half-eaten heart!
O, the yellow locks beside thee
　That I often kissed and curled—
Yet no hell-fire will betide thee
　In the waste beyond the world.

Tiger, tiger! from the sod,
  And the vastitudes of sea,
Thou wert molded by the God
  Who in glory molded me:
Ashes, dust and air and fire
  Entered in our earthly frame—
Went to kindle my desire,
  Went to fan thee into flame.

Tiger, tiger! blazing bright
  Are thine eyeballs as mine own—
They the darkness and the light
  Of revolving suns have known;
They have seen the jeweled June-light
  Sleeping in magnolia blooms,
Seen the weird, mid-winter moonlight
  Shivering by solemn tombs.

Tiger, tiger! though thy frame
  Is unlike my mortal parts,
Yet the feelings are the same
  That have flashed within our hearts;
For thy blood hath leap'd with passion,
  Languished with a strange unrest,
And thy hatreds are in fashion
  With the hatreds in my breast.

Tiger, tiger! this is why
  Thou hast slain my brave, sweet son.
Yet the good God up on high
  Let the devil-deed be done.
Atoms from far, countless places
  Met and mingled in thy form,
Dust of old, dead realms and races—
  Memories of sun and storm.

Tiger, tiger! from the flood
  And the cloud and wind and lea,

Atoms mingled in my blood,
  And the lost boy bloomed for me;
And these forces—separated
  By infinities of years—
Met, and left me desolated
  In   their   death-march   through   the
    spheres.

Tiger, tiger! he was mine—
  He, the beautiful dead boy!
Now thine eyeballs swim and shine
  With a strange and savage joy;
And I see thy keen claws dripping
  With the blood that warmed his breast,
And I hear thy hot lips sipping
  From the lips that mine have pressed.

Tiger, tiger! I can see,
  Slipping through the jungle dim,
One who is beloved of thee,
  And thou art beloved of him;
Ay, beloved, for thou begat him,
  Just as I begat my boy,
And I see thee pet and pat him
  With a sweet and savage joy.

Tiger, tiger! twangs my bow,
  Flies my arrow through the air,
And the golden lilies glow
  With his life-blood leaping there;
And I hear thy wild, quick, pleading
  Cry of passion and of pain,
And I see thee press the bleeding
  Body of thy baby slain.

Tiger, tiger! this is life:
  Through the wide sweep of the spheres
All the universe is rife

With these tragedies and tears;
And the gladdest song upswelling
From the gayest heart to-day
Brings it nearer to the knelling
And the coffin-worm and clay.

COMPENSATION

They say I am mad, ha, ha! because
 I see the visions they cannot see,
And—breaking through all of their little laws—
 I walk with the lover who went from me.

Mad? mad? ha, ha! if they only knew
 How happy I've been since that strange far
 year,
When I found that I had been born anew
 To a larger life and sublimer sphere!

When was it? Oh, yes,—I remember now,
 In a dim. vague way that I saw his face,
With a dash of blood on his darling brow,
 And a glad, sweet smile of immortal grace.

Then all of their vulgar world went out,
 While the turbulent bells in the steeples beat,
And thrilled and thundered the song and shout
 Of the crazy crowd in the stormy street:

And, as I staggered, before that blank
 Lost feeling insensate befell me, I
Heard pealing over the city rank
 And rotten the virulent victor-cry!

They found me there when the mob had left,
  And they bound me there and they brought
    me here;
But though of my reason I am bereft
  I live and love in a larger sphere.

Ah! Leon! Leon! you come again!
  I was telling this clown that you   came   to
    me—
A very miracle man of men
  In our sphere serene which he cannot see.

Let us take a walk down yon aisle of trees
  Where the almonds are blossoming full   and
    fair,
And a voyage over the golden seas
  To the glory of which he is unaware.

Stand back, oh, fool! From this cell I go
  With my dead to divinest heights. Ha! ha!
If you only knew what we mad folk know
  You could bring the world into abject awe.

But you cannot know it. We are a clan
  Who have broken through all of your laws,
    and we
Hear miracle things that you never can—
  See miracle sights that you cannot see!

VASHTI

O, I feel the fragrant wind and I hear the waters
     sing,
I see the sweet, wild roses blushing with the
     blood of spring,
And the world leaps up to heaven as I hold
     thee to my breast
In a swoon of perfect rapture, with a sense of
     perfect rest.
          But I waken with a start,
          And my torn and bleeding heart
Cries unto Christ: "Have pity—let my soul
     and senses part!"

There cometh no reply, and I rise and look
     abroad:
It seemeth that the whole wide world hath
     turned away from God—
Its garlands of glad forests that fringed the
     stainless sky,
Its foamy lilies and the flame of tulips closer
     by,
          Its prairie-lands uncurled
          To the edges of the world,
Where trilled the tuneful wild-birds with their
     jewel wings unfurled.

Yes! The night hath swallowed up all the
     beauty and the bloom;
Our planet reels and rolls away through awful
     gulfs of gloom;
Within the lone, black, shuddering void the
     lost winds call and cry,

And from its craggy rim the sea makes piteous
    reply:
        Fit symbol and fit sign,
        O, heart—O, heart of mine!
This fierce, complaining passion to the passion
    that is thine!

I turn. The fire burns bright—with rosy rise
    and fall
It lights a pure, seraphic face upon the pictured
    wall;
O, Vashti! Vashti! Thou wert love and hope
    and life to me—
Then come from out the vague Unknown and
    take me unto thee.
        Bliss—bliss ineffable,
        Divine with thee to dwell
Upon the white calm heights of heaven or in
    the heart of hell!

In the radiant rose-years of my bright and
    buoyant youth,
When my life was lapped in pleasure and
    my world was masked in truth,
When with color, life and melody the jocund
    days were rife,
Like a dream of heaven made real came thy
    love into my life.
        In that witching world of mine
        Was no separating line
Between my heaven and the heaven where
    saints triumphant shine.

But this was not for long—a wild March morn-
    ing came
That woke no song within the wood nor touched
    our star with flame,
And thou in thy fair bridal robes lay still and

Within thy blood no fire, within thy folded
    lids no light.
        Why was it ordered so
        That I thy love must know
For one brief diamond day and then forever-
    more forego?

Unjust! unjust! I hold, for the world is wide—
    is wide;
Why should I with thy love be dowered to
    have it thus denied?
Out of the infinite of Time, the vastitudes of
    Space,
O, why should Fate foreorder it that we meet
    face to face?
        Why swept no seas between
        Thy way and mine, my queen?
Why lay no long-drawn centuries betwixt our
    lives terrene?

O, had I never seen thy fair, sweet Southern
    face,
Nor folded thee in ecstasy within my fond em-
    brace,
How happy would have been my heart that now
    is crucified,
How full of flower every hope that with thee
    drooped and died!
        Why was it ordered so?
        It was not chance, I know.
It was a Curse that rules the world, and ruins
    all below!

But, look! the storm is stilled, and there is no
    more night.
The shining signals of the morn move on from
    height to height;

The glory of the gods shine through the blue,
  rtanslucent sky,
And vineyard, field and flood lift up a jubilant,
  sweet cry.
      O, heart—O, heart of mine!
      Is it symbol, is it sign
Of a resurrection morning that will ransom
  thee and thine?

WHAT IS THE USE ?

What is the use of it all?—I said,
  As we sat in the argent after-glow—
All are dying who are not dead,
  And unto the end it will be so.

Love; but the one whom you love will pass
  In blooming beauty, some dark, mad day,
To fatten the grave-worms under the grass:
  Yet this is a jolly old world, you say!

Build; and the temple you build will fall—
  Frieze and pillar and altar-stone
Over its ruins will reptiles crawl,
  And the ivy wave in the winds that moan.

Work; and the gold that you work to
    win
  That you fret and worry and strive to
    save
Is spent in folly and shame and sin
  When you are dust in a dreamless grave.

Capture the laurel-leaves of fame
  Where they bourgeon out of the blood of
    men;
Conquer a nimbus for your name
  By the miracle-power of the pen;

But the garlands of glory will fade away
  And thy name be lost in the dim, dumb
    years:
Where are the heroes ere Adam's day—
  Their flaming thoughts and their flash-
    ing spears?

They prate of a phantom-world afar,
  Beyond the mold and the marble urn,
Beyond the fire of the furthest star,
  Where life is immortal and love eterne.

But I am no dupe of their priestly dreams;
  They know of nothing that is to be;
The light that out of their heaven streams
  Is the self-same light that shines on me.

I hear the voices they hear, and I
  See every sign that they behold,
But dumb as death is the stainless sky,
  Invisible are the gates of gold.

Thro' the sum and sweep of the countless
    years,
  Humbly at many a countless shrine,
Men and women have wept their tears,
  Or quaffed to the lees communion wine;

But never a gleam of glory fell
  In splendor athwart the altar-stone,
And never a sound but the passing-bell,
  Smiting the air with its awful tone.

They have stormed the stars with their
        passion-cry
For hope or mercy or justice here—
Plead that their darlings should never
        die—
Plead with many a sob and tear.

Folly! for never an answer came,
    And never an arrow was turned away;
It sped to its beautiful mark the same,
    Whether they prayed or scorned to pray.

From cradle to coffin we struggle and seek,
    Till the fugitive years of our lives are
        past;
But whether our lot be blessèd or bleak,
    We are tossed like dogs to the worms at
        last.

What is the use of it all, I say?
    Why are we brought from the blank Un-
        known
To weep and dance through a little day
    That drifts us under a burial-stone?

AGATHA

Agatha!
Agatha!
Here in the desolate shadows and silence
        I cry unto thee,
    As out of the bloomland
    That was, and the tombland
That is, comes the ghost of thy glory to me!

I see a vague vision elysian, of flowery
  fields and of forests that know me
  no more.
O, trancefulest thyland!
Memorial myland!
How far I have wandered away from thy
  shore!

The low yellow moon of the June in the
  purple abysm of heaven-lit tower and
  tree,
As there in thy splendorful,
Wistful and tenderful
Beauty my soul was surrendered to thee.

Agatha!
Agatha!
There in the moonlight that flickered and
  flashed through each blossomy bough,
  With breast to my breast, sweet,
  In raptureful rest, sweet,
Thy virgin lips uttered the infinite vow.

Mine, mine in thy truthful,
Brave, questionless, youthful
Devotion, till death threw its portals ajar;
Mine, mine in the vernal
Sun-valleys supernal,
Beyond the pale shroud and the palpitant
  star!
But the battle-drums beat, and I bade thee
  farewell
  To fight for a rag of a flag, and a cause
  That had its roots down in the under-
  most hell,
  And its flowers and fruits were the lies
  we call laws!
Ah! I was a fool in that far-away time,

Mistaught to believe in the sham and the
　　shame
That in code and in charter have crystal-
　　lized crime,
To blossom in blood and to flower in flame.

Like devils we fought a fell, desperate fight,
Till our vexil in victory flashed on the height
Of the last shattered bulwark, and then, with
　　my sword
Uplifted to heaven, I knelt to the Lord—
I knelt to the Lord on that wild battle-plain
Beside a dead youth that my rifle had slain—
Beside a dead youth—with a sharp, sudden cry
I turned the bright brow from the dust to the
　　sky.

O, God, with a terrible thunderbolt smite
Me out of thy love and thy life and thy light!
It was Agatha!—clad in the garments of war:
In her hand was a sword—on her shoulder a
　　star—
In her breast was the bullet my rifle had sped—
The bullet that struck my whole universe dead!

THE VANISHING ISLE

Under the willows, the glad green willows,
　　We walked that hour in June—in June—
And the songs of the breezes and birds and
　　billows
Were all in tune.

　　"Ah, see!" cried Ion, with subtle smile.

"Yon isle—yon blossoming, blissful isle!"
And she waved her little white hand to
    where
Magnolias tossed in the amber air,
On the strand of an isle that idly lay
In the pulsing heart of the purple bay,
Where palaces lifted their walls of gold
And jeweled minarets; and, behold,
The peerless parterres that are all afire
With flowers that ravish the last desire!

"Boatman!" she said, and she crossed his
    hand
With gold as she gave him the strange
    command,
"Boatman! O, let us taste awhile
The rare delights of yon charmful isle."

'Nay, damosel, for that isle lies
In an alien land under alien skies,
And we cannot reach it before the doom
Has swept us all to the tomb—the tomb!"

"Pah!" and she cheerily laughed, "a mile
Will see us there on the tranceful isle."

"Then come!" said the boatman. And we
    went
Through the miracle morn that was inter-
    blent
With sunbeams, over the waters bright
And blue, in a spell of rapt delight.
Ah, miracle morn! Our hearts beat high
With love—with a wonderful love—and I
Was ravished with jubilant joy—for, O,
    Her promise was mine and her presence
        sweet
    Made life in its largest mood complete—
For I loved her so! For I loved her so!

Noon came; but the isle was far away
In the pulsing heart of the purple bay.
I looked at Ion: her face was wan
And wrinkles under her eyes were drawn,
And half of her life was gone—was gone!

Dusk; but the isle was far away
In the pulsing heart of the purple bay;
And a storm swept up from the under-sea
  With trumps of thunder and flags of flame;
I turned to Ion. And was it she
  Who mumbled to me—was she the same
Bright, buoyant maid of the golden morn—
This woman haggard and gray and worn?

I turned to the boatman and, lo! for he
Was dead, and his bare skull grinned at
    me—
Grinned in a devilish kind of way;
And the isle—the vanishing isle—lay
Long, terrible leagues away—away!

INEZ

Through the mists of the roses as red as wine
I see the splendor of sunset shine;
It brightens the blossoming valley and leaps
To the ultimate snows on the vapory steeps;
While over the hills in the occident skies
The walls of a wonderful city rise.

   *   *   *   *   *   *

Out of this convent dim some day
I shall pass to that place away--away;

I shall meet with my warrior bright and brave
Who perished the shrine of the Prince to save.

* * * * * *

Years of splendor and storm have passed
Since I prest the lips of my lover last—
Since over the waste of the sand and sea
He went in the dark, wild dawn from me,
With shining helmet and sable plume
To meet on the red war-plain his doom.

* * * * * *

One night of thunder and wind there came
A palmer weary and old and lame,
And kneeling in homage beside me there
He gave me a glittering lock of hair,
A jeweled picture, a jasmine flower
That once had blossomed within my bower.
"He is dead?" I spake with a rush of tears
That blotted the sunshine from out my years.
"Yes, ladye, yes but he sent with me
These emblems of endless love to thee!"

* * * * * *

I turned with a low, heart-broken moan
To kneel by the cold, pale altar-stone,
Until, through the oriel window old,
The morning blossomed in blue and gold;
And then, while clashed the cathedral bell,
I wailed to the world a fond farewell:
Farewell, O, beautiful marble towers!
Farewell, O, gardens of glowing flowers!
Farewell, O, waltzers and songs and wine!
Farewell, O, musical lyre mine!
Farewell, O, friends in thy joy and mirth!
Farewell, O, pitiful pomps of earth!
I renounce ye all for the convent dim
And the heavenly city that holdeth him!"

* * * * * *

What! did he die for a nameless sin
And not by the lances of Saladin?
Shall I on the heights of the holy dwell
While he writhes in the uttermost pits of hell?
Shall eternity sever my love and me?
By the Holy Rood, it shall never be!
Out in the depths of the wicked town,
Where they trample the roses of purity down,
I will sell myself to the lusts of men!
I will riot in many a gilded den!
I will curse the Lord with my latest breath
As I rot away in the arms of Death!
Deep in the outer darkness then
He will clasp me close to his breast again,
And hell shall a perfect Paradise be
Unto the soul of my soul and me!

PATRIOTISM

I would not lift my hand to stay
    One flag up-floating in the skies;
They all are symbols of a sway
    That hath its root in leprous lies.

This patriot talk, this puerile talk
    Of duty done with blade and brand,
These badges for the brave who balk
    The fell invaders of a land,

Are hollow mockeries; the old
    Hell-fire burns in every cause;
The few find glory, place and gold,
    And make and minister the laws;

What time the many who have borne
The heat and burden of the fray
Are left—though poor and bullet-torn—
The debt and sacrifice to pay.

And though the lamps of Science shine
Illuminant from zone to zone,
And though the race in ransomed line,
Files up at last unto its throne,

And though we boast of conquests higher
In Truth than our forefathers knew,
We still are slaves unto desire,
With blood our hands we still imbrue.

My harp shall strike a higher key
Than lust or blasting battle-call,
And though no after-bards there be
To follow where my foot-prints fall,

Yet I will know that I have sought
To help and royalize my race,
And lift it from the wrath and rot
Into a glory and a grace!

HAROLD

What do you think since your day has come,
And she takes you tenderly by the hand,
And you find that your lips are forever dumb,
Though your heart is sobbing to say farewell,
Ere you journey off from this lower land
To the land of which travelers never tell?

What do you think as you hear her cries
And the cries of your children blent in one?—

As you look in the depths of their darling eyes,
   And know that you never again will meet,
That your labor and love and life are done
   And the uttermost measure is incomplete?

Do you think that you did the diviner part
   In wooing a wife in your rare rose-years—
Knowing your heart from her loving heart
   Would sooner or later be torn away—
Be torn away, while the bloody tears
   Of a last despair would be hers some day?

Do you think it was god-like to give the flame
   And passion of life to your children fair,
Knowing through sorrow, or want, or shame,
   They would pass to the greedy grave at last
And surfeit the red-throat reptiles there
   When this wild drama is overpast?

O, fool! fool! fool! Since the passion-spell
   And pleasure of love are leaving now,
Where is the song of the bridal-bell,
   The scent of the bridal-lilies sweet,
The bliss of the bridal-chamber vow
   In the shadow white of the winding-sheet?

Behold! She is bending beside you now,
   And storming the Gates of God with prayer;
The bridal blossoms upon her brow
   To stinging serpents have turned to-day,
Her rapture has turned to a mad despair
   As you drift o'er the dim, still seas away.

Behold your children! To them you gave
   The pitiless curse and cross of life—
The duty to struggle and dree and slave—
   They must tread on the plow-shares red with
      fire,

Their hearts must break in the bloody strife,
    They must pant in the toils of a vain desire.

They may reach their hands for the splendid
        stars,
    For the laurel-leaf and the princely plume,
They may ride at last in their victor-cars,
    And then, in the proud, sweet flush of fame,
Be swept like dogs to the dirty tomb
    To rot like the ruffian spawn of shame.

Or, failing to realize the dreams
    That gilded with glory this lying life,
They will turn to a beautiful sin that seems
    A recompense for their lost desire.
Who will be guilty? The man and wife
    Who gave to these beings their blood and fire.

Reproach me not in your dying-hour,
    I told you the truth in my friendship leal,
But, held in the spell of a subtle power,
    You mocked at me then with a scoff and
        sneer;
To-day the terrible truth you feel—
    Its thorny crown and its savage spear.

Farewell! No further will I upbraid,
    Nor seek revenge by returning now
The bitter and biting things you said
    When under the stars of Tennessee
You spake of your silly betrothal-vow
    And turned like a traitor then from me—

Turned like a traitor, because I plead
    With you to recall your betrothal-ring;
Turned like a traitor, because I said
    That life should end with our race to-day:
You spurned me then like a leper thing,
    And passed to this awful fate away.

*   *   *   *   *

HE IS DEAD! Well, better that he should die,
And under the myrtle-blossoms be,
Than live and, living, should learn what I
   Have learned of his boy, whose hands are red
With the blood of a dead man known to me.
Thank God! My Harold is dead—is dead!

GEORGE ELIOT

We crowned her brow the queen of such wide fame
  As seldom man's more ardent thoughts hath wooed;
But still our hearts were heavy for the shame
  She wrought to womanhood.
                    —*Literary World.*

O, knave! O, more than knave!
  Why should she bear the brand?
    And why proclaim
    Her sin and shame
  From land to furthest land,

While men of leprous lust
  With harlots hold their court,
    And wear the bays
    Through all their days
  Undimmed by ill-report?

And hath this sin a sex?
  And shall we bar the gate
    To maiden who
    Hath proved untrue
  And fallen from her state,

What time we welcome in
  The man who wrought her woe?

No, never, by
  The God on high,
With me shall this be so!

George Eliot, no peer
  Of thine will hiss thy name:
    'Twill brighter burn
    Through years eterne,
Though devil-prudes defame.

I hold this truth as true,
  All love is lust at best;
    No mumbling priest
    Nor wedding-feast
Things beastly can make blest.

And though no bridal-bell
  Chimed in thy coupled life,
    Thou art as free
    Of stain as she
Who hath become a wife.

Though Church and State befool,
  Me they cannot bedaff;
    I strip their lies
    Of all disguise,
While in my sleeve I laugh.

I laugh when I behold
  The bridegroom and the bride
    At altar-shrine,
    By sleek divine
With ring and pledge allied.

For well, full well, I know
  That passion hath full sway
    Behind the flush
    And modest blush
That o'er their features play.

And were no sexual fire
  Within our veins, I see
    That nevermore
    On sea or shore
  Would any weddings be.

And louder still I laugh
  When to a wedded pair
    A babe is born:
    The mask is torn
  Forever from them there;

And forth they stand confessed
  Of all their sly delights,
    The same that they
    In mansions gay
  And guilty take o' nights.

Thus, though the world o'erlaid
  With gloss and glitter be,
    They cannot hide
    The under-side
  Of life and love from me.

GERALDINE OF THE GRAEME

The silvery lances of twilight fall
  In the roses tangled around my sill,
And over the green, old garden-wall
    The jasmines shine and the jasmines
      spill.

The beck is babbling a summer song
  As it bubbles over the sand and stone;

The wind blows sweet and the wind blows
    strong
From   waves   unseen   and from   wilds
    unknown.

And out of the purple south away,
    With a love as tender as love can be,
In the magic light of the dying day
    My bold, bright Carolyn comes to me.
*   *   *   *   *
The red moon rose over trees and towers,
    And staggered under a cloud with shame,
And the wind sobbed low in the ferns and
    flowers—
    Sobbed low for Geraldine of the Graeme.

Then with a terrible trumpet-peal
    It summoned the storms from the fur·
    thest skies,
And the sea swirled over the sand and
    sheal,
    And answered aback with its curdling
    cries.

Tree and turret and river and rock
    Glared for a moment and then were gone
In the titan-smite of a thunder shock,
    Like the crack of chaos at judgment-
    dawn.

But over the storm that split the sky,
    And over its clangor on sod and sea,
Was heard a long, wild, pitiful cry:
    "My daughter—my daughter!   O where
    is she?"
*   *   *   *   *
Laughing and leaping through rose and dew
    The miracle morning comes once more;

Never before was the sky so blue,
And never the world so fair before.

The rain-drops ripple from turf and tree,
And quiver and quiver with hearts of
fire,
And daintily over the leaf and lea
The zephyrs hang with a sweet desire.

The lark is winging and warbling up
Out of the grass through the golden air;
Lily to lily waves its cup
And drinks of dew to the roses rare.

Sing the fountains and shines the flood—
Shines the grass and the greenwoods
sing—
But, hold! for here is a trail of blood!
And here, O, Christ! her betrothal-ring!

*   *   *   *   *

A sunken grave in a churchyard gray,
A handful of dust, a dishonored name,
And a wan, white phantom that walks,
they say,
Through the dim, old rooms of the
haunted Graeme.

*   *   *   *   *

But Carolyn sits in his pomp and pride,
To-day, in a splendid hall of state;
His wife and children are by his side
And crowds of courtiers upon him wait.

They know that he lured her down to doom
With lies as crafty as lies can be;
But what do they care, in that gilded room,
Where they revel and dance and jest in
glee?

What do they care? He is a man,
And woman is always a proper prey;
It has been so since the world began,
And thus will forever be, they say.

DOROTHY

I stand on the windy headland where we stood
    in the yester-years;
I gaze on our green, low valley through the
    blur of my burning tears,
And think of a slain September afar in a pulse-
    less past—
A beautiful, brave September that was too
    bright to last.
O, Dorothy! O, my Dorothy! it was here that
    I met with thee
One balmy and brilliant morning that was far
    too blest to be—
One fairy and fateful morning, with never a
    voice to warn,
As up to the very heavens the soul of myself
    was borne.

I see thee now in the splendor and flush of thy
    flowery youth—
Serene in thy witching beauty, supreme in thy
    matchless truth;
And all through that brief September—the
    briefest my life hath known—
I reveled in maddest rapture, for thou wert
    mine now—mine own.

Then jealousy came between us with whispers
    I cannot name.
O, fall on me, rocks and mountains, for I was
    alone to blame—
For I, in my reckless anger, spake sharply a
    last farewell,
And plunged from the highest heaven to the
    deepest deeps of hell!
      *   *   *   *   *
Over the world I wandered, from zone to the
    furthest zone,
Till I knew all the pains and passions that
    ever to man were known—
Had seen all the mystic marvels of nature in
    noblest guise;
Had stood in the grandest temples that tower
    beneath the skies;

Had met with the mightiest leaders of life in
    this lower sphere,
But, ah! through it all, belovèd, my heart was
    forever here.
And now that the calm September hath come
    to our world once more
I stand on the windy headland where we stood
    in the years of yore;   .

I gaze on the green, low valley, unchanged
    since I saw it last,
Save out of its sweet seclusion the self of my-
    self hath passed,
Save out of its sweet seclusion the soul of my
    soul hath fled.
O Dorothy!—O my darling!—art thou dead,
    and forever dead?
      *   *   *   *   *   *
Ah! who is that woman standing down there by
    the rocky shore?

She seems like a dream made real from radiant days of yore;
The grace of her every motion, the tint of her
gleaming hair—
I surely have seen that woman—have seen her
—but when and where?

And why are my pulses leaping as they leapt
that September tide
Before the desire of living from out of my life
had died?
O, Jesu! it is my belovèd!—O, Jesu! it is my
bride!

* * * * * * *

He ran down the cliff and, turning, she stood
transfixed, while he
Caught her close in a stormy passion of a joy
too vast to be.
"Speak! speak!" he panted. "O darling! the
desolate years have passed.
And I—I have come to claim thee—at last—O,
my love!—at last!"

He staggered and fell—a bullet had cloven his
heart in twain.
"Ha! ha!" laughed the woman loudly, "my
waiting was not in vain!"
And to-day in a grim old mad-house she glee-
fully clanks her chain.

KENNETH, MY KING

Thy marvelous beauty, my blue-eyed boy,
  Shines starry-like through the lurid years,
Till I flush with the old, fierce, fetterless joy,
  Forgetful of time and tears.

As I saw thee then I can see thee now:
  The passionful love on thy perfect face,
The golden locks on thy brave, white brow
  Tossed back with a nameless grace.

And, holding thy harp in thy slim, white
    hands—
  Ah! the harp and the hands are but dust
    to-day—
I hear thee sweeping its silvery strands
  In thy own wild, peerless way.

Spell-bound I listen until it seems
  That I live in the light of thy love once
    more,
And revel in all of the strange, sweet dreams
  That never fruition bore;

And my dead hopes rise from their funeral
    pyres
  As blessed and beautiful as of old;
And high in my heart spring the sacred fires
  That never were quenched nor cold.

O, Kenneth, my king! I joyfully cry,
  Stretching my arms to thy vision there
To clasp it close to my heart— but I
  Clasp only the empty air!

And I waken again to the awful truth,
  As black and bitter as truth can be,
That heaven was lost in my hapless youth,
  Belovèd, in losing thee.

Yet if unsealing thy coffin-lid
  I could bring thee back with one old, fond
    kiss
On thy beautiful face, I would forbid
  Myself the infinite bliss.

For sweeter by far is the dumb, blank rest
  In thy windowless palace beneath the sod,
Than life in a world where life at best
  Is only a fleeting fraud—

Is only a fugitive fraud, where friends
  Clasp hands and sever with sad farewells,
Where the jubilant bridal or banquet ends
  In the moan of the funeral-bells.

KING CUSTOM

I have heard men bravely brag
  That our land at least is free—
Heard them say our star-lit flag
  Symbolizes liberty.
But they knew their lips were lying—
  Knew that they were shackled slaves
Of a monarch, whose undying
  Power tracks them to their graves.

Custom is that monarch. He
  Sways the Church and Camp and Court,

Makes and molds society,
  Enters into every sport,
And he sets the silly fashions
  Of the men and women folk,
And he bringeth all the passions
  Underneath his iron yoke.

Though a hand from heaven sows
  Seeds that sprout and spring to vines,
Bearing fruit that gleams and glows
  With its joyous wealth of wines,
If ye quaff the red, ripe juices—
  Grown and given for use of man—
Custom, without terms or truces,
  Forthwith brings you under ban.

If you hold yourself aloof
  From the mob, you soon will hear
Custom crying: "This is proof
  That the man is cracked and queer."
Then he summons up his rabble,
  And he winks to them their cue,
And, with smirk or curse, they gabble
  That their master speaketh true.

If belief should leave your soul,
  The belief in creed and church,
If you question their control,
  If you leave them in the lurch,
If you lift your eyes to Reason
  As the pole-star of the world,
Custom shrieks out, "Treason! treason!"
  And his shaft at you is hurled.

If your taste is pure and high,
  All undimmed by things below,
If you, with a calm, cold eye,
  Look on life's vainglorious show,

See no beauty in the faces
  Nor the forms of womankind,
To their vaunted gifts and graces
  Are by nature wholly blind—

Then King Custom with a hiss,
  Like a serpent in your track,
Howls unto his mob at this,
  And they hiss and howl aback;
And how quick they be to utter
  False surmise in whispers loud;
And how swift they be to mutter
  Things as vulgar as the crowd!

Thus King Custom holdeth sway
  Over all our hills and plains;
Many long to break away
  From his mandates and his chain
But they weakly fear and falter
  At the wrath that would await,
So they ponder and they palter,
  And submit unto their fate.

Unto this King Custom I.
  Never will my homage yield;
His decrees I will defy
  Till my sepulcher is sealed;
I will own no other master
  Than the good God over all,
Though it doom me to disaster
  Till the final shadows fall.

IDALIA

"O, follow, follow me!" cried Love, as in the
    jasper skies
The morning pearled, and made the world a
    perfect Paradise—
The morning pearled: its vexile flashed, and
    flamed its victor blades,
As back it drove the darkness from the glad
    heights and the glades.

"O, follow, follow me!" cried Love. Idalia fol-
    lowed where
He led her, through the low, sweet fields of
    asphodel, and there
The larks rained down their golden song from
    out the purple air.

He led her through the vineyards where the
    blue grape-clusters hung,
And through the dewy pleasaunce where the
    crimson roses swung,
And the yellow-winged canaries in the olean
    ders sung,
And life was like a fairy-tale, and all the world
    was young.

And on and on she followed, till they came
    unto a land
Where a river clanged forever through a wild,
    weird waste of sand—
Through the rushes clanged forever, and the
    blinding sunlight shone
On a serpent, coiled and hissing, by a ruined
    altar-stone.

And on and on he led her, though her bleeding
    footprints showed
That the cruel rocks had torn her as she jour-
    neyed on the road;
And on and on she followed, till the Darkness
    came once more,
Camping with its conquering legions on the
    sea and on the shore.

Where was now the brave, bright Morning?
    Where were now its swords of fire?
Where were now its sweet delusions? Where
    was now its strong desire?
Cold and dumb and stark forever doth its
    bleeding body lie,
And its proud, imperial banners shine no
    longer in the sky;
While the Darkness—drunk with triumph—
    calls the Tempest o'er the rim
Of the under world, to riot in fierce revelry
    with him.

"Love, where are you?" sighs Idalia, but there
    cometh no reply:
Tears the wind across the desert, dash the
    cloud-racks through the sky,
And the lightning hurls its lances, and the
    thunder-drums beat high.

"Love, where are you?" cries Idalia, as she
    sinks upon her track;
"Love, where are you?" sobs Idalia, but he
    sends no answer back;
"Love, where are you?" shrieks Idalia. From
    the ruined altar-stone
Comes a curdling peal of laughter, ending in
    an awful moan;

And a skeleton reels forward; there is cypress
    on its brow,
And a ring upon its finger; and it cries: "As I
    am now
Will you be, O, poor, lost maiden! for you fol-
    lowed Love away;
For you followed Love who leadeth hither only
    to betray;
For you followed Love, who lureth only to de-
    sert at last,
When the first fresh dew and blossom of our
    beauty is o'erpast.
I was once a bonny lassie in a glad, green land
    away;
Through the dear old household places I went
    singing all the day;
But Love sought me as a victim, and I ven-
    tured in his train,
And I gave to him a jewel that I never might
    regain;
Then there came a few sweet moments of mad
    rapture, but no more
Was the world, or life, or heaven, what they
    always were before;
Still I followed him, and followed, under many
    a stranger sky,
Till he left me here—deserted—in an hour like
    this—to die."
      *   *   *   *   *
She is lying where the river clangs through
    rushes sere and brown,
With the ring of her betrothal that had brought
    no bridal-crown—
Where the river clangs forever with a warning
    under-tone,
Where the serpent coils and hisses by the
    ruined altar-stone.

Over her the vultures hover, and with talons
    keen they tear
From her face, and limbs and bosom all the
    beauty that was there,
Till her skeleton lies bleaching in that desert
    dim and bare.

With her little babe beside her that had never
    breathed of life,
There they find the poor, lost mother who had
    never been a wife—
There they find her, where the river clangs
    forever through the sand—
Only one of many maidens lured into that aw-
    ful land.

THE SOLITUDE OF SELF

The loneliest thing in this lonely sphere
    Is self, in its prison of flesh and bone ;
Between the closest of comrades here
    Is a wall as thick as a wall of stone.

There are thoughts we think that we cannot
    tell
    To any being of woman born,
For the fetters of language they repel
    And spurn with a proud, quick, reckless
    scorn.

Eyes cannot express, nor touch translate,
    The dreams refulgent that come to me ;
Nor the burning love, nor the blasting hate,
    Nor the truths supreme that my soul can
    see.

When skies at sundown are splashed with fire
    A vivified vision mine eyes behold,
And I look with a look of a rapt desire
    On castles of glory and cliffs of gold,

Where seas of jasper in jewels break
    On shoals of beauty and shores of bloom,
Where never and never a heart shall ache,
    On the awful verge of an open tomb.

I try to mutter the thoughts that come
    To me in the hush of the half-light then;
But, ah! for my lips are dumb, and dumb
    To me are the lips of my fellow-men.

No matter if I should cry and call
    Till my tones went tingling unto the stars,
Man could not hear me—for, O, the wall
    Between us forever! It bars—it bars!

And thus when I struggle my love to speak,
    Its infinite secret I cannot name—·
For words are pulseless and cold and weak,
    And wanting the force of the vital flame.

And so with the eloquent hate eterne
    That I have and hold for the whelps of
        wrong—
Its fell, fierce fury I cannot burn
    And brand in the brain of the brutish
        throng.

I cannot tell them the strong, sublime
    Contempt I feel for their laws, ah, me!
For vicious virtue, and Christian crime,
    And serf·hood singing that it is free.

I cannot impart the immortal flame
    Of the truths I own to these churlish clods

Who sanctify every sham and shame,
And say they were given them by their gods.

Thus lonely, ah! lonely, each wends his way
To the shadows and silence, and never
    knows
The souls that walk with him day by day
To the restful palace and last repose.

GUITEAU

I

I will sing a song that never brother-bard hath
    sung to thee,
For the spirit of its rhythm is revealed alone
    to me.
May be on the heights of Heaven seraphs sing
    it to their lyres,
May be in the depths of Hades devils shriek it
    in the fires;
But I know not, and ye know not; hearken to
    its hopeless strain,
And deny it or defy it, still its ripened truths
    remain:

II

Nothing is that is not ordered by an over-rul-
    ing Power,
From the master march of planets to the soft
    fringe of a flower:
We are nothing more than puppets, and this
    Power pulls the string,

5

Making of that man a menial, making of this
    clown a king;
Models one in manly beauty, perfect he in
    every part,
Great in mind, and grand, majestic, in the im-
    pulse of his heart,
Marvelous, serene and lofty, born the masses to
    command
With a look, a tone, a motion of his white,
    bejeweled hand.
He, the stately one and saintly, seldom feels
    the spur of sin,
And can stay it and suppress it by the master
    will within;
His are gold and love and glory, and the
    faith that sees afar
An unending life of rapture o'er the blue rim
    of our star.

III

But behold a fellow-mortal fashioned on an-
    other plan:
Coarse, deformed, and misbegotten—more a
    devil than a man—
Heir to sin and want and sorrow, born with-
    out a sense of shame,
Stung by sharp, keen, fierce desires burning in
    his blood like flame;
Weak, unbalanced and repulsive—reveling in
    sensual things,
If he hath a soul within him 'tis a soul that
    never sings—
'Tis a soul that hath no wings!
If he speeds the blasting bullet through the
    heart of fellow-man,
Blameless he, for it was bidden when the uni-
    verse began;

He was born without the power or the impulse
    to forbear
When the dumb, resistless forces of the cycles
    centered there;
That which gave him life had given passions
    that impelled him here;
Circled him with strong temptations from his
    birth-cry to his bier;
Formed the hour and circumstances; placed
    the pistol in his hand,
But withheld the strength and schooling his
    impulses to command.

IV

Nothing is that is not ordered by an over-rul-
    ing Power,
From the master-march of planets to the soft
    fringe of a flower;
From the Charity that standeth with its sunny
    wings unfurled,
While her white hands shower blessings and
    her sweet lips kiss the world,
Unto Crime, with bloody bullet, flaming torch
    and dripping blade,
Stalking over tombs and ruins his destroying
    hand has made.
If athrough the mists phantasmal with the saints
    we walk in rhyme,
If our hearts are set to music of a melody sub-
    lime,
If we wade with knife and fagot through the
    blood our hands have spilt,
From that Power came our glory, from that
    Power came our guilt.

DE PROFUNDIS

Where the singing groves of summer glittered
 in the crystal calm,
 Wave the black, funereal branches, O, so
  bleakly! to and fro;
Where the blithe, capricious linnet poured its
 pure, impassioned psalm
 In the bright syringa bushes, drifts the deso-
  lating snow;
While the harvest-twinkling hill-tops—traced
 on the translucent blue
In the splendor-hearted summer—fade in spectral fogs from view,
And the wan, wild dusk descendeth over trees
 and tarns away,
As I think of friends departed in and out the
 grave to-day.

Over seas and over sand-wastes some upon the
 earth-plane still
 Think of thee, O, poor, proud spirit! beat-
  ing at thy prison-bars;
Of the old time by the yule-log, when the
 Christmas blasts blew chill,
 Or in cool, calm groves, green-raftered, where
  the roses shone like stars!
Dear hearts! nevermore to know thee—never-
 more—O, dark decree,
Thus to meet one merry season, but to sepa-
 rated be:
Better thrid the thorns unfriended by the
 throngs of thoughtless men
Than to meet the true and tender thus to weep
 farewells again!

68

Underneath the waving willows in the calm,
    old kirkyard low,
  Some are dreamless dust forever, as our-
    selves at last will be;
Yet this life of flowers and feasting is the only
    life we'll know,
  And this life of pain and parting is the only
    hell we'll see.
Wo! I saw the waxen cere-cloths, wet with un-
    availing tears;
Wo! I saw the funeral torches flaming by their
    plume-proud biers;
Thus the dismal yester-shadows dim the sun-
    shine of to-day;
Ah, if Memory could perish, Misery would
    pass away!

Fate, O, Fate! Why mock and madden us with
    beautiful, bright eyes,
  With loose locks of golden glory, and with
    wine-red, winning lips,
With cool, creamy arms that clasp us in a per-
    fect Paradise—
  Then the vivid, saintly vision let the coffin-
    lid eclipse?
Better never live, O, mortal!—thus I hold with
    bated breath—
Than to drop into the darkness, ah, so desolate,
    of death;
Better never love, I whisper in my wickedness
    once more,
Than to see our idols shattered at the shrines
    where we adore!

BRITOMARTE

It was not much that I implored of **Fate**:
I did not ask for bays to crown my brow;
I did not ask for gold to gild my home;
I did not ask for liberty from toil;
Nay, none of these were plead for in my prayer;
And yet the one sweet blessing that I craved
Has been denied me by my destiny.
I only asked that I might have a friend,
Whose looks would lighten when he saw my
    face,
Whose voice would soften when he spake to
    me,
Whose hand would tremble, when he took my
    hand,
With thrills of bliss because it pressed my
    palm;
Who would not see my faults—would only see
My better self, all unobscured by sin;
Who would not hearken to the tongue that told
Of rumors dark concerning me or mine:
A friend indeed, and not a summer friend
Whose smile was mine while sunshine, too, was
    mine;
But one whose thoughts of tenderness would
    rise
And deepen and proclaim themselves, when
    time
Of storm and wreck and midnight came to me.

I now am old and weak and near my tomb,
But neither in the glorious capitals,
Nor yet within the hamlets hidden far

From the mad, jarring world in greenwoods
    dim,
Have I beheld a woman or a man
Who was possessed of an unchanging heart.

I have met those who came to me, and by
Their gentle smiles and gracious words have
    won
Their way into the center of my soul,
And then deserted me and left despair,
All crowned and sceptered, on the very throne
Made vacant by their treachery to me.

Take one as an example of them all:
I see him yet, a tall and handsome boy,
With golden locks that glinted in the sun,
With eyes like violets, whose depths within
Sparkle the dew-drops at the dawn of day.
His face was like in color to the bloom
Of apple-blossoms: just a hint of pink
Seen through the snowy whiteness—that was
    all.
He said his love was mine, and then he made
My love his own, until I worshiped him
Blindly and madly, and I would have gone
With songs of gladness through the flood or
    flame
To serve him, if thereby I could have made
Him happy as his fond vows made myself.

Then, wo! there came a time when leagues of
    space
And lengths of seasons lay between us both;
But we had spanned the great gulf with our
    pens,
And over this frail bridge did we transmit
Devoted messages.

But the hour struck
When there were no responses sent to me.
A black and awful silence fell between
Us both; and moons of winter shuddered by,
And moons of summer blossomed in the blue,
And still no word—not one poor syllable
Was heard from him.

　　　　At last I knew it all;
Knew that he had renounced me; that no more,
Here or hereafter, would our pathways cross.
He flung me back my love, and with it flung
His scorn and scoffs.

　　　　O, God! O, God! I thought—
Kneeling prone down within my lampless
　　　room —
What have I done that I should thus be hurt--
Be trod upon like reptile in the dust?
That, too, by one of all the others best,
Most dearly loved and reverenced by me!
There were no tears within mine eyes, ah, no!
Great grief can never thus be washed away,
There were no moans within that chambered
　　　gloom—
Only the dumbness of a last despair!
The night passed on, and lightning split the
　　` sky;
The night passed on, and horrid thunders
　　　clashed;
The night passed on, and rioted the rain;
The night passed on and morning broke at last,
Broke for the world, but never broke for me!
The cloud, the tempest, and the darkness still,
Of that fierce night remain within my breast.

He was the last of all my friends, the last
Lone love to which I clung, and he had proved
As faithless as the rest.

Without one cause,
One reason rendered, he had thus betrayed
My trust in him.

And I had loved him so!
Heaven! O, heaven! I had loved him so!
I have withdrawn from all humanity,
Foresworn my kind and live for self alone.
Yourself can be a friend unto yourself
Through loss and pain and utter lack of hope:
All other friendships are but mockeries.
Follow them up and you will surely find
That, like the jack-o'-lantern of the moor,
They will but lead you to your ruin down.

THE SONG OF HATE

Come I at last, my masters! Come I at last,
    though late,
To sing in your ears, unwilling, the terrible
    Song of Hate—
A Song that will startle the timid and make
    them tremble and pale;
        But the truth I seek,
        And the truth I speak,
Though the whole world cower and quail.

Hate I that World, my masters, with all of its
    show and sham;
Its masks and lies and illusions, deceiving us
    but to damn;
I heartily hate the living and I hate the very
    dead,
        And everything

By vassal or king
That ever was done or said.

For since the first fierce morning of Time, with
    its toils and tears,
Down through the dim, long vista of fleet and
    fugitive years,
I see but the one black picture 'twixt cradle
    and coffin-bed,
Of conquering knaves,
And cowering slaves,
And the doom that struck them dead.

Hate I that World, my masters, so given to
    shame and sin,
Where mortals by Fate are hobbled and fet-
    tered and hampered in;
And never I moan nor marvel, when I hear the
    curdling cry
Of wretches who dare,
In this hopeless snare,
To curse their God and die.

Hate I the name of Pleasure; it is ever akin
    to pain,
And leaves a poison to rankle in spirit and
    heart and brain;
Whenever it droppeth a lily adown on my sun-
    less path,
I shiver with fear,
For I know that anear
There hurtles a bolt of wrath.

Hate I the name of Friendship, of all things
    fickle and frail,
For, O, in the time of trial full oft have I
    seen it fail;
And if it be fond and faithful, then only too
    well I know

It will wither and pass,
Like flowers and grass,
When the winds of the death-day blow.

Hate I the garish bauble of Fame, that gilded
    cheat!
It schooleth the glib-tongued rabble in the
    lessons of deceit;
Down would they bow before me, if I were
    chosen chief,
        Though I won the race
        Through my own disgrace
To the place of a titled thief.

Hate I the name of Riches, they bring in their
    blasting train
A rout of covetous courtiers who fawn at thy
    feet for gain;
Nothing they care, O, nabob, for thee, it is
    plain to tell;
        Name them in thy will
        For a sum—then spill
Thy blood. It will please them well.

Hate I this Life, my masters, so cruel and calm
    and cold;
Hate I the awful Secret that never to man was
    told!—
The mystery speechless and silent, that wraps
    us around and about,
        That sealeth the tomb
        With a ghastly gloom,
And shutteth the future out.

Hate I it All, my masters, but most I hate
    Mankind;
They are deaf to the voice of counsel, to their
    plainest duty blind;

I cry, and they scoff my warning, I call, and
      they only jeer;
            While they laugh and scheme
            In a rosy dream,
Till Azrael makes them hear.

UNSUNG

            O, that mystic song!
            O, that mystic song!
It is hunting and haunting me down my days
      with its melody sweet and strong!
      The splendor of suns is in its strain,
And the tinkle and tune of the wide blue waves.
And the flash of the rainbows through the
      rain,
And the glory of life, and the light of graves.
      While songs of heaven and shrieks of hell
      Are one in its surging underswell!

            O, that magic song!
            O, that magic song!
It blends the vices of mortal right with the virt-
      ues of mortal wrong;
      It sets to music the serpent's hiss
In time with the singer's lute; it blends
      In rarest rhythm our bale and bliss,
And curse of foemen and kiss of friends,
      While the feet of the demi-gods keep time
      With the tramp of devils adown its rhyme!

            O, that subtle song!
            O, that subtle song!

I strive and struggle to vivify and voice it un-
  to the thoughtless throng;
But though it burns in my blood to-night,
And sings and sings in my mind to me,
  Its miracle words I may not write,
Nor utter its secret sense to thee;
  It slips the leash of my language when
  I seek to pinion it with my pen!

      O, that spirit song!
      O, that spirit song!
Only to me of our mortal race its melody doth
  belong;
  Yet, O! if I might unlock its bars,
And O! if its music I might set free,
  My race would walk on the shining stars
Forever in company with me,
  And my fame would thunder from zone to
  zone,
Till Time lay dead on its golden throne!

A PROPHECY

" And ever will right come uppermost,
And ever will justice be done."—*Charles Mackay.*

A lie! a lie! a glittering lie!
  Though set to a sounding strain,
While roystering princes revel high
  And their vassals clank the chain.

A cheat! a cheat! a glorious cheat!
  While Virtue cries for bread,
And Vice is battened on banquet meat,
  And quaffs of her wine rose-red!

Look forth! look forth over all the lands,
  And what do thine eyes behold?
Guilt, holding a scepter in gory hands
  And wearing a crown of gold;

While Innocence toils in the mart and mine
  And taxes its frugal hoard,
To pay for the purple and linen fine
  And the pleasures of its lord.

"And ever will right come uppermost,
  And ever will justice be done!"
A boast! the false and the frivolous boast
  Of a knave and a fool in one.

Rise high on the rounds unto power and
    place
  By felony, force and fraud,
And history hides thy dark disgrace,
  While every land will laud.

Be true to the trust of the dead who die
  For the Truth—it forever fails,
And its base betrayer will pass thee by
  While thy motive he assails.

"And ever will right come uppermost,
  And ever will justice be done!"
A boast! the damned and deluding boast
  Of a knave and a fool in one,

Who would flatter the meek mob on to
    think
  That a distant day will bring
To the humblest toiler the meat and drink
  And the fine robe of a king,

And make them forget their galling gyves,
  And turn to their tasks again,

And work and worry through all their lives
  For the profit of princely men.

But never will right come uppermost,
  And never will justice be done,
Unless there rises an awful host
  Some day beneath the sun,

And dooms its kings to the bloody block,
  Their palaces to the flame,
And breaks every fetter and yoke and lock
  That binds it to its shame;

And burns in a bonfire every page
  Of the laws that rule to-day—
That had their root in an ancient age
  When savages held the sway.

But, mark the prophecy!—mark it well!
  That time we will never know;
Forever the Strong will buy and sell
  The Weak—it is ordered so;

And never will right come uppermost,
  And never will justice be done,
Till we sail away from this mortal coast
  From under this mortal sun!

PRESENTIMENT

The night was a night of June
  As I sat at my window-sill
And sang to the shattered moon
  In tune with the whip-poor-will.

Then out of the future came
  A mystical feeling. I
Shrank back with a sense of shame
  And a low, swift, frenzied cry;

For I knew there was coming soon
  A terror too vast for me,
And I prayed to the broken moon
  That glittered on sod and sea.

The morning pearled at last
  In melody, dew and bloom,
But I shuddered as one aghast
  On the edge of his early tomb.

It was never a fear of death
  That dirled through my spirit. Nay:
It was something that came by stealth
  To walk with me day by day;

And my high and my haughty scorning
  Went down in the dust, and I,
In the light of that lovely morning,
  Died deaths you can never die.

For they brought her unto me; then
  With a laugh they left her. O, Christ!
A thing to be shunned of men—
  For her soul had been sacrificed!

"My girl! O, my beautiful Grace!"
  I raved in a last despair,
And I stung her sovereign face
  With my passionful kisses there.

She lived for a little while,
  And then she was only clay—
Besmirched by the grime and guile
  Of a devil she met one day;

And out on yon windy wold
Is her dreamless dust to-night,
And here I sit, in the gold
And the gleam of the firelight.

* * * * *

There cometh unto us all
A knowledge of things to be,
And agonies that appall
Forever I can foresee.

AVERY MERIWETHER

Born, July, 1857. Died, July, 1883.

My Avery is dead,
In the sunflash of his life—
Dead in the sunflash of his love; and the world
with its roses rife!—
Yea, the world with its mocking roses rife and
swimming in the wide
Blue sky—o'er-brimming with song, as if our
dead had never died.

My Avery is dead!—   ·
The dear boy went from me
With a loving. look on his pure, pale face that
I never more will see,
And rivers and rocks and leagues of land be-
tween us lay waste and wide,
But I said: "I will see him again some day,"
and I said it while he died!

My Avery is dead!
Low in the Southern dust
Is the hand that gave with a generous will, and
 the heart forever just,
And the thoughts that scaled to the very stars
 —unwritten as yet for man,
And every beautiful dream, and hope, and de-
 sire, and wish, and plan.

O, Nature, calm and cold!
O, Nature, why is this?—
Why summon us out of the dumb, bare void
 to a little day of bliss—
To meet with the great, sweet, generous friends
 like the friend whom I weep to-day,
Then sever us far as star from star in this mad,
 unmerciful way?

Gifted with genius high,
Unselfish and pure and brave,
O, why should he go in his glad rose-years to
 rest where the lilies wave,
While the guilty whose garments are splashed
 with shame, live on in their slimy sin
Till their hair is grizzled, before the grave
 will open to let them in?

But Avery still lives,
Though clad in cerements chill;
In the works he wrought, in the truths he
 taught, I know he is living still—
Is part of the miracle woods and waves and
 the sky and the stars to-day,
For the soul thrills out through the universe
 when the senses fade away.

Is it unconscious there?
Shall it never know us, when

We slip the leash of our bondage here, and
    drift from the days of men—
Drift out through the infinite sweeps of space
    on the surge of immortal years,
And melt in the mighty universe through all
    of its suns and spheres?

        Nay, nay, it cannot be!—
        In ways to the wise unknown,
We will feel and know, as we felt and knew
    before our breath had flown,
Though we melt in the mighty universe till the
    endless end shall be,
And live in the spray of the singing waves and
    the blossom on the tree.

        Why should the tear-drops burn
        Our eyeballs at his tomb?
Why should we hide our faces there where the
    ferns and the flowers bloom?
It is only a little, little while till the last of
    us all shall go
Out over the rim of the radiant sky, and know
    what our dear dead know!

        Only a little while—
        O, why did Avery die?
This cold philosophy cannot hush our hearts'
    poor, pleading cry;
O, why must he go in his glory-time with many
    a wreath unwon
That was growing to garland his pure, proud
    brow with a splendor like the sun?
        *   *   *   *   *
        O, Life! O, Death! O, Time!
        O, World! O, dark, unknown,
Mysterious, speechless void on void with peo-
    pled planets sown!—

Ye only serve to feed the worm that crawls
    within the tomb,
And blast forevermore a hope when in its
    brightest bloom!

    O, why should it be so?
    O, what—what have we done
That we are summoned from the void to live
    beneath the sun—
To live and cheated be with hopes that turn
    to serpents here;
To see the bridal-blossoms droop and wither
    on the bier;

    To feel the loving hand
    Turn icy in our own:
To cry farewells that cannot reach into the dim
    Unknown;
To feel the stab of perfidy, the sorrow and the
    pain,
The yearnings never realized, the rasping of
    the chain;

    To know that life will end
    End in the murk and mold
Before the song is half-way sung, the tale is
    half-way told?
O, pitiless! O, pitiless the God, the Law, the
    Fate,
The Nature—call it what you list—that ruleth
    our estate!

    O, Avery! my Avery!
    The day is half-divine,
The sod is all a-blooming and the sky is all
    a-shine,
And the flash and song and fragrance of the
    summer green and gay,
Mock laughingly at Death and all that Death
    has done this day!

Insensibly there comes
A sweet, triumphant thought
That somewhere in the Universe a Truth is left
   untaught—
A Truth that will unriddle all the mysteries that
   be
And let thy soul electrify our souls eternally!

CRESENTIUS

Behold him as he stands—
The chains upon his hands
The noblest and the knightliest one in all the
   Roman lands!

On his black charger he
Had led to victory
Ten thousand thousand Romans through the
   battle's din and dree.

Then streamed his war-plume white,
Gleamed in the golden light
His mail and helmet, bearing deep the dints
   of many a fight.

Now, cruel rack and wheel,
His flesh is made to feel,
But, lo! his true, unmurmuring lips no secret
   will reveal.

Behold his quivering frame'
Behold the proud, calm flame
Within his eagle eye, the while they taunt his
   naked shame,

And break his battle-sword,
That for themselves hath poured
The blood of foemen where the flag of Rome
imperial soared!

"Step forth!" The headsman leads,
And, though each fiber bleeds,
Cresentius goes with grand, high mien   to die
for noble deeds.

With bright, unbandaged eye
Doth he the ax defy,
While bending to its bloody stroke . . . a
mad, quick tiger-cry

Leaps from the people there—
Rage, pathos and despair
Are blended in the awful wail that breaks up-
on the air.

Thus, in a devil-age,
Was the historic page
Splashed with the blood of men who threw at
tyranny the gage.

Thus did they dree and die
On block, or cross-tree high,
Because the hell-whelps on the throne they
boldly did defy.
And though the rack and wheel,
And though the headsman's steel,
No man within our boastful land hath yet been
made to feel,

Still, if we dare defy
A mailed and mitered lie
Of Church or State, its tools will **hate and**
hound us till we die.

NO PLACE FOR ME

The dancers dance in the palace-halls to the
　mad, sweet music there,
While I stand outside of the ancient walls in
　a passion of despair;
Bubbles the red, red Orient wine, and quiver
　　the creamy blooms,
While scintillant jewels sparkle and shine
　down all of the princely rooms;
I hear the persiflage blithe and bright and the
　rippling laughter free,
But, O! wherever a heart is light, there is no
　place for me.

I stand on a mountain ledge, and lo! a city
　before me lies—
I see its western windows glow in the flame of
　the sunset skies;
And I think of the happy homes where wait
　the tenderful hearts and true—
Of the welcoming kisses at the gate, in the
　roses and the dew;
The laughing lips and the eyes impearled by
　sympathy I see,
And I sigh to myself: In all the world, no
　home has a place for me!

I tread the turbulent streets and I full many a
　face behold—
I watch them carelessly pass me by, with
　calm, proud looks and cold.
They never dream, and they never will, how I
　long their love to know,

How their beautiful eyes make my pulses thrill
    as they did in the long ago;
I pass, and my lips with pride are curled; none
    shall my misery see,
But I cry to myself: In all the world no heart
    has a place for me!

I see full many triumphant spheres of dignity
    and renown;
Here clash the warriors' clanging spears, there
    sparkles the victor's crown;
Here the poet sings, and the world is hushed
    to listen unto his lays,

There the statesman stands with his honors
    flushed, in the splendor of his days;
But whether in sphere or high or low, on the
    shore or on the sea,
No rich reward will I ever know: There is no
    place for me!

Be brave, O, heart! There's a place of graves
    afar in a lovely land,
Where murmur the long, blue Mexic waves up
    Mississippi's strand;
And there through the silvery summer-tide the
    oleanders bloom,
And drift their red, sweet flowers wide o'er
    many a nameless tomb;
And there, when my life is overpast, in the
    beautiful years to be,
I will find a rapturous rest at last: In the
    grave is a place for me!

MELODIES OF MISOGAMY

LIONEL LA VERE

Lionel La Vere was standing by the passionate,
  pale sea,
Where it broke in magic murmurs on the craggy coast of Lee,
While the orient was shining with sun-lances
  light and long
As the new day flashed upon him with its fragrance, dew and song.
He, the glorious and gifted, with his poet-
  sense could see
A new earth and a new heaven on the lovely
  coast of Lee;
And his soul rhymed with the morning; with
  a rapturous outcry
Lifted he a glad hosanna to the purple sweep
  of sky—
Lifted he a glad hosanna foɩ the life that
  seemed so fair;
For the sweet, resplendent visions that were
  circled 'round him there;
For the friends whose deep devotion never
  yet to fail was known;
For the Hopes that marched before him with a
  splendor all their own—
Hopes that lifted high their torches, beck'ning
  down the future dim,
Pointing to the victor-laurels that were blossoming for him;
For the grand All-hail Hereafter, far beyond
  the stars and sod,
When his mortal race was over and he rounded
  back to God.

Thus, with jubilant thanksgiving did he dream
    of years to be
On that miracle young morning by the singing
    summer sea.

Moons have toiled down into darkness since
    that morning kissed his brow—
In the dust and roar and tumult of a city is
    he now,
Struggling with his fellow-beings in a battle
    for his bread,
In despair ofttimes upcrying, "O, to heaven
    I were dead!"
All the joyful flush and splendor of his youth
    have passed away;
Golden mornings cannot thrill him as they did
    in that old day,
And his blood no longer tingles with a riotous
    delight
When a sylvan scene transplendent blooms in
    beauty on his sight,
For he sees beyond its beauty, and "It is a
    mask," he cries,
"To a rotten world that reeketh with its lepro-
    sies and lies!"
Slowly did he learn the lesson, that the world
    he deemed so fair
Crucified its Christs forever—placed its Pilates
    in the chair;
That it cursed the Right forever, and forever
    crowned the Wrong,
Keeping for the weak its shackles and its scep-
    ters for the strong.
He had held a creed progressive—pure as star-
    fire of the skies—

Held a creed that turned and trampled on all
　　leprosics and lies;
But the rabble rose in anger and assailed him,
　　for they saw
That behind their savage statutes was a whiter,
　　holier law,
And they hated its Apostle, for he tore their
　　masks away,
And revealed their rank pollution to the dazzle
　　of the day.
One by one his friends forsook him— fearful of
　　the public wrath—
Leaving him to fight the foemen crowding clos-
　　er in his path.
Thus he learned his first sad lesson: Friend-
　　ship is an idle tale
And thy friends will all assail thee, if the world
　　shall first assail.
One by one his Hopes fell dying; darker still
　　the world became.
Where were now their blazing torches that had
　　cheered him with their flame?
Where were now the victor-laurels they had
　　promised long ago?
Where were now the love and friendship they
　　had told him he should know?
Vanished—like the lovely vision of a dear, dead
　　face in sleep
Rising from beneath the roses, leaving us to
　　wake and weep.

Years march on with shout and laughter, while
　　with red, right hands they slay
Brave and beautiful and brilliant men and wo-
　　men by the way;

Years march on with shout and laughter, beat
  ing down into the grave
All the rosy dreams and pleasures that their
  predecessors gave.
Lionel once more is standing on the lonely
  coast of Lee,
Broken-hearted now and haggard, looking o'er
  a stormy sea;
And a wan, white mist is crawling over tree
  and tarn afar
As the dark day moans and shudders to a night
  without a star.
"I will put my trust in heaven!" thus he cried;
  then, mockingly,
Laughed the very winds on-sweeping, frowned
  the sky and hissed the sea,
Until universal Nature to his fancy took a
  tongue,
Crying, "O, poor fool! you trusted in this world
  when you were young;
It was brave and great and tender, and it filled
  your grand ideal,
So you trusted it, and found it hollow, treacherous, unreal.
"If the Maker made a swindle of this world
  and life and time,
Will he keep the golden promise in a gladder
  sphere sublime?
Fool, that you have ever trusted—greater fool
  to trust again
In a vague, phantasmal country pictured out
  by priestly men.
Never downward from his bastions rang an an
  swer to a prayer,
And no God has ever spoken from his glory
  over there,

And no lips have ever opened on which Samæl
  set his seal,
Any hint or any whisper of its raptures to reveal.
It is all a feeble fiction. Trust in nothing save
  a rest
That will round through ceaseless cycles in
  the clammy earth's cold breast."

*
* *

Lionel La Vere is rotting underneath the white
  rose-tree
Where he spake his glad hosannas, on the
  craggy coast of Lee.
Ruined dreams, betrayed affections, faith evan-
  ished, were his lot,
Yet the sea sings on beside him, and of man
  he is forgot—
Yet the sea sings on beside him, shines the
  sun and flash the flowers,
And the wild-birds wing and twitter in the free
  and fragrant bowers,
And the mad world booms and thunders in its
  passion and its pride,
And men laugh and dance and marry as if he
  had never died.
Nature counts the dead as nothing, and she
  frolics o'er his rest,
While red-throated worms hold riot on the
  heart within his breast—
Hold the riot and the revel they will hold o'er
  all at last,
When the dream and disappointment of our
  lives are overpast.

*
* *

We may laugh and dance and marry—dally
  with a soft romance—

Still the Doom runs through the cycles; we're
    the sport and fools of Chance.
And to-day we lift the beaker where the ban-
    quet-board is spread,
But to-morrow we are wailing by the white
    face of our dead;
And to-day we hear the trumpet pealing forth
    our names with pride,
But to-morrow by the people we are speared
    and crucified;
And to-day our friends caress us, hold us
    closely to the heart,
But to-morrow they desert us, while they speed
    the poisoned dart.
This is life—and though its sunrise beautiful
    and blest appears,
Soon or late it dips and darkens into ashes,
    blood and tears;
Yet the Church, and State, and People, pander-
    ing to their passions, cry,
"It is good—a thing of glory! Wed, increase
    and multiply!
It is good—a thing of glory! Wed, increase and
    multiply!"

BLESSINGS OF BACHERLORHOOD

The happiest life that ever was led,
Is never to woo and never to wed.
              —Old Song.

HAL

Say, Cecil, old fellow, unless you take care
You will be an old bachelor—here is a hair
That I've pulled from your bonny, brown
    tresses, and, lo!—

You may look for yourself,—it is whiter than
  snow;
And, Cecil, a sly little wrinkle I trace
On your temple—the first of a ravaging race
That will ruin the roses of boyhood—
                    CECIL
                              O, tush!
Quit your bother—I'm busy.
                    HAL
                    No, no; I won't hush;
You are thirty, unwedded, and, what is a shame,
You haven't a single sweetheart to your name,
And so, on the whole, Bud, your prospect is
  blue,
And I think it high time I was talking to you.
                    CECIL
Tut! Fiddlesticks, boy! Take a glass of this
  wine—
I think you will find it uncommonly fine.
You won't let me finish my writing, I see,
So light a havana and listen to me:
Let others go marry for all that I care,
I never will do such a thing, I declare;
And thus will I save myself many a woe
That the poor, hapless Benedict only may know.
I'm foot-loose, unhampered by woman or child,
I'm free as yon bird that flits merry and wild:
I rise in the morning whenever I list,
I stay out at night and I never am missed,
I come or I tarry whenever I choose,
I smoke or I drink when I'm down with the
  blues,
And there's none to complain or control me,
  my boy,
As I revel and dance through a lifetime of joy.
When I come to my snug, little sanctum I
  know

That a fire is blazing with cheeriest glow,
My pipe and my papers are ready for me,
And the walnuts and wine when I've finished
    my tea.
Grand company's waiting for me, I well know—
Shakespeare, and Byron, and Shelley, and Poe,
And all the great bards who have brightened
    the earth
With words of sweet wisdom, and pathos, and
    mirth;
With these for my comrades I well can re-
    nounce
The presence of furbelow, ribbon and flounce,
While the cry of a tearful and troublesome child
In the lap of its mother would worry me wild.

HAL

But love?

CECIL

I have fond, faithful friends, as you see,
And their kindness and care is sufficient for
    me.
We are bound by no tie save the tie of the
    heart;
No scandal would sully our names should we
    part;
If I tire of them or they tire of me
We can utter adieus and forever are free.
Not so with a wife.

HAL

No; but then the bright joy
Of a bosom-companion to live with, my boy;
Who would offer wise counsel, and help you,
    and cheer
Your upward advances from year unto year;
Who would crown you her king, with a wo-
    manly pride;

"Who would double your joys and your sorrows
divide."

CECIL

The picture is pretty, but very unreal,
Like a sculptor's white vision, a poet's ideal;
The helpmate you paint I might possibly find,
But the Fates might decree a far different kind;
And what if the woman whose ways I adore
Should tear off a mask when the marriage is
o'er,
And show me a nature, harsh, vulgar and cold,
A meddlesome spy or a petulant scold?
Why, Hal, it would drive me distracted, and I
Would take up my hat, and would bid her
good-bye;
Then lawsuit and scandal would fall to my
share,
And the shame would be more than my spirit
could bear.

HAL

Is that it, old Cecil? Now, listen to me;
If your wife should be all that you fear she
would be,
You would find compensation, bright, tender
and sweet
In your children—without them no life is complete.

CECIL

My children! Now hearken, and heed what I
say,
I would rather be dead than a father to-day;
Aye, rather by far, for temptations are spread
At each corner and step of the way that we
tread,
And my children might bring on my house and
my name
The dark, crimson blotch of unspeakable shame.

HAL

But if they were all you would have them to
    be?

CECIL

No matter,—I never of fear would be free.
Day and night, night and day, I would dread
    that the doom
Of the grave would sweep over their glorious
    bloom,
And leave me bereft in the blaze of my years
With a fierce, hopeless future of terror and
    tears.

HAL

Time would heal.

CECIL

                Never, never! I think you declare
Your belief in the Bible?

HAL

Yes, yes..

CECIL

                        You have there
Learned the lesson that only the souls of the
    blest
Will wing their white way to the raptures of
    rest;
Yea, only "a remnant" be saved, it is said
While the multitude, marching on down to the
    dead,
Will pass through the portals of time and the
    tomb
To suffer and shriek in dominions of doom
Forever and ever; and how could I tell
That no child of my house would sink into this
    hell,
And leave me the thought that in granting him
    breath
I had given him likewise damnation and death?

*   *   *   *   *

O, the red-throated worms must rejoice when
   they hear
The bridal-bells chiming all cheery and clear,
And the heart of old Lucifer tingle with pride
Whenever he looks on a bridegroom and bride;
For isn't it plain until weddings have ceased
That the red-throated worms are assured of a
   feast?
That Lucifer still will have souls to destroy,
While weddings replenish our planet, my boy?

THE SECRET OF THE SONG

Cecil:

O, sing me a song, Llewellyn, that you sang
   in that lost, lost June,
When the robins swung in the roses, and car-
   oled and chirped in tune—
When your life was a life of rapture, and your
   love was a love whose fire
Had lent to your lays the gladness of a great,
   ripe, sweet desire.
I know she is dead, Llewellyn, I know she is
   dead to you,
Or proved like a swikeful siren to your beautiful truth untrue—
And you in that mad, vast moment were turned
   to a cynic cold,
And never again, ah, never! will be as you
   were of old!

Llewellyn:

Ha! ha! my comrade romantic! Now, really I
· hate to say
Your charmingly fond compassion is utterly
thrown away;
The woman you speak of, Cecil, she never has
pricked my pride
By proving unleal to her pledges, and I know
that she never died—
Nay, never, my dear old fellow, for she never
has yet been born
To harrow my heart by dying or ruffle my
wrath with scorn.

Cecil:

Then why do you sing, Llewellyn, of love and
of love alone,
That lieth under the star-light and the dim
old burial-stone;
Or false to its first free passion; or answerless
—unattained;
Or living in gilded splendor with all of its
glory stained?
Why do you sing, Llewellyn, in rhythm and
rhyme so real
That people think you are singing a song that
your soul must feel?

Llewellyn:

Because I have seen the passion, because I
have seen the pain,
Of bright young lovers a-weeping, and wringing their hands in vain—
One for a sweet bride, sleeping low under the
cypress bough;
One for the traitor hearted who trampled upon
his vow;

One for a love above him, as stars are above
the sod;
One for a pure, proud woman transformed to a
painted bawd;
And I cried to myself: O, cruel! yea, cruel is
love as hell,
And lost is the poor, weak human subdued by
its subtle spell,
For, though it be fast and faithful, its funeral-
bell will ring,
And over its cold, white ashes the grasses of
May will spring—
Will spring in the golden sun-flash, while the
bleeding heart will cry
For pity unto a Ruler who never hath made
reply.
The bards in a grand procession have gone
through this world of ours—
Gone singing its songs and sky-flash, and the
pomp of its purple flowers:
The splendor of great, white mornings, the
glory of twilight time,
And the miracle Soul behind it, supernal, su-
preme, sublime;
Gone singing the love of lovers—its gladness
too deep, divine,
To intercommune its essence by subtlest of
speech or sign;
Gone singing its touch mesmeric, its tremors
that flame and flush
In kisses and last caresses that blend with the
bridal-blush;
And the folliful lads and lasses have listened
unto the lays,
And twined the betrothal blossoms in the rose-
tide of their days,
Belured by the strain seductive, and led to the
dark, last doom—

For the path that leads to the altar leads on to
the awful tomb—
The tomb of the little children who are born
of the bridal vow,
And the tomb of the wife and husband, so
happy and hopeful now.
Though Perfidy sheathe its dagger, and though
Pride stoops down to kiss,
Thus vanishes out forever the vision of bridal-
bliss.
This is my answer, comrade, my answer to all,
for I
Feel pity—a keen, quick pity as a wedding-train
sweeps by:
Bright are the sparkling jewels and white are
the dancing plumes,
Gay are the bells up-chiming and sweet are
the golden blooms,
Merry the rippling laughter and rosy with sweet
delight
The dream of a flashing future and the bliss
of the bridal night;
But I, from my calm, cold vantage, forethink
of the future hours
When the crest of a hooded serpent will lift
through the orange-flowers—
When the gulf of the grave will open and the
funeral-bell will knoll,
And the radiant dream will vanish with the
flash of a flying soul.
Though the passions and tears and moaning
of Love are in my strain,
I never have known its pleasures, I never have
known its pain;
I sing from a heart that pulses in pity for all
my race
Who kneel in the dust and worship the charm
of its devil-face;

And if from my lyre leapeth a song that will
  save the youth
In the flush of their manly beauty and the flame
  of their manly truth,
I will thrill with a glad thanksgiving, and cry
  with a victor cry:
I am greater than God—the greatest—up there
  in the sunny sky!

CLAUDE

It was night, and the nimbus that circled the
  moon
  Forespoke of the storm that the morrow
    would bring:
A witch-dog was barking down by the lagoon
  That lay in the forest—a festering thing;

The wind whuddered loud and the wind whud-
    dered low,
  And puffed the white dust down the high-
    way in whirls,
And whipped the bare boughs of the trees to
    and fro,
  And whisked up the froth of the bayou in
    skirls;

When up the old road, trending off to the right
  Of Sherwood, and skirting the Darrell
    domain,
Came a man with a bundle and stick through
    the night,
  And he walked as though weary with hunger
    and pain.

Claude Darrell, the bonny young lord of the
    Hall,
Was down at the ivy-hung lodge-gate alone—
He was straight as an arrow and graceful and
    tall,
And handsome as any young god on a throne.

He saw the old man and he cried, "Where-
    away?"
And the traveler slowed up his steps as he
    said :
My boy, I have tramped since the dawning
    of day—
Can't you help an old man to a mouthful
    and bed?"

"Ta-ta!" said the boy, with a curl of his lip,
    "I don't pension beggars. Ta-ta, sir! Don't
    lag."
The man with his stick hit the bundle a clip,
    And cried, "I'm no beggar. There's coin in
    that bag."

"'The case being altered, it alters the case,'"
    Said the youth, with a keen, rasping ring
    in his tones;
"Come in! I have food, and old wine, and a
    place
Where to-night you can sleep off the ache
    in your bones."

So the old man went in and the youth served
    him well,
And after their supper they smoked for a-
    while,
Till the hour of ten rang its rusty, old bell,
    And the host showed his guest unto bed
    with a smile.

There was none in the house save the boy and
the man,
And a scowling old servitor, deaf as the
dead.
* * *
It was said that the youth was the last of his
clan,
And out of his fingers his fortune had fled.

A rake and a reveler ere he was twenty,
His riches had rapidly taken their flight;
His houses and lands were all mortgaged. A
cent he
Had not when he met with the graybeard
that night.
* * *
The clock clanged the hour of one from the
wall:
Claude Darrell rose up from his seat by the
fire,
And, taking a candle, he crept through the
hall,
And up the old stairs he climbed higher and
higher

To the room where he knew the old man was
reposing.
* * *
With a knife in his hand and with hell in his
heart,
He turned back the door-knob. The old man
was dozing,
But straightway awoke with a shudder and
start.

"Claude Darrell!" he shrieked, as he sprang
from the bed

And seized the young man with a furious
   hold,
"A half-minute more. and I would have been
   dead,
  For you thought through my gore you would
    capture my gold.

"I dreamed you were coming. The dream has
   come true—
  For a few paltry dollars your soul you would
    damn!
O! what have I done that this punishment's
   due?
  Claude Darrell! O, Claude! you don't know
    who I am;

"For you were a baby when long, long ago
  I sailed o'er the seas in my bonny young
    years:
There came a great tempest, and far on a low
  Rock, our vessel was wrecked off the coast
    of Algiers.

"We were captured, and there in a slave-market
   sold;
  Year crawled after year, and I found myself
    free;
But I heard that low under the myrtle and
   mold
  My wife and my baby slept here by the sea.

"So I never came back until now. In the mart
  Of the tropics I piled up great treasures of
    gold;
For merrily Fortune will smile when the heart
  On the world and its trappings no longer has
    hold.

Then I heard that my boy was still living,
     and, O!
It swept me to heaven! No saint in the sky
Feels a bliss like the blisses that surged to
     and fro
In my heart as I said to myself: 'By and
     by

" 'I will meet with my baby—my beautiful
     one,
With his mother's blue eyes, and her ringlets
     of gold—
O, I wish—for my dream is forever undone—
That I lay with her under the myrtle and
     mold!

I said to myself as I sailed o'er the sea:
'I will go in the garb of a tramp to the Hall,
For I know that a mouthful and bed there will
     be,
As there was in the past, for whoever may
     call;

'And when I have rested the crick in my back,
And tested my son with a fatherly pride,
And cheered myself up with a bit of a snack,
As he tells to my face how his old father
     died,

"I will quit my disguising, and taking my boy
To my heart, I will tell him that he is my son,
And, O! how I pictured his passionate joy
When he found that myself and his father
     were one!

What—what have I done that my sweet
     dream should lie
In its blood at my feet? Is it just—is it just

That a Tri-headed Tyrant should sit in the sky
  To mock and bedevil us worms of the dust?

"Claude Darrell, I came to the Hall, but you
    know
  The rest of the pitiful story, my son—
The rest of the pitiful story, for O!
  My beautiful babe and Claude Darrell are
    one!"

As if stricken to stone—voiceless, pallid and
    cold,
  With a horror that darkened within his deep
    eyes,
The youth had stood still till the story was
    told,
  Then he tore himself loose with loud, maniac
    cries;

He sprang through the door, down the stair-
    way he fled,
  And out of the manor, and under the moon,
On—on, as though driven by devils he sped
  Till he came to the edge of the awful lagoon.

His father had followed him into the night,
  But never a trace of him there could he
    see:
He called, "O, come back to me, Claude, and
    in spite
Of the past thy old father will idolize thee!"

But never an answer came back to his ears
  As he ran up and down through the Darrell
    domain,
And sought for his son, while the blistering
    tears
  Blurred his loving old eyes, but the search
    was in vain—

But the search was in vain till the desolate
morn
In its dark thunder-garments walked over
the world,
And wailed for the radiant things that are born,
And then to the red-throated reptiles are
hurled.

Then the father saw foot-prints. He followed
them fast
Through the pleasaunce and meadows and
forest-lands bare—
He followed them far till they vanished at last
By the lonely lagoon. With a cry of despair

And a clutch at his throat he sank down on the
sod,
For under the water he saw a white face,
And he cried, "O, my Claude! O, my beautiful
Claude!
And thus dies the last of my long, princely
race!

"O, had I but known in the folly of youth
What I know in the wrinkle and gray of my
life—
Had I caught but one gleam of the glorious
truth
With which the whole universe ever is rife,

"Ah, I would have thwarted the Fates and
their fell,
Blasting fury, for Claude would have never
been born,
Nor would I be feeling the fires of hell
As I look on his dead face this desolate
morn!

"The King Curse of Curses that walk through
    the world,
  Is Wedlock! O, would that its rings and its
    flowers,
Its vows and its altars forever were hurled
  Into darkness eterne from this planet of
    ours!'

POEMS OF PASSING MOODS

PANTHEISM

I sing not of this changeful clime—chaos of
    sunlight and of snows—
But of the deathless summer-time in land of
    lily and of rose,

Where, boating in the breathless calms upon
    the lotus-purpled Nile,
We drift between the regal palms and pyramids
    for many a mile.

Here, where the viper rears its brood within the
    noxious weeds and flowers,
A pillared city proudly stood with golden min-
    arets and towers.

Behold this lone, deserted place, where serpents
    thrid the tropic-grass,
Here, in its stateliness and grace, a kiosk stood
    of stone and brass;

But now the night-bat and the owl hide in its
    poison-reeking vines,
And jackals and hyenas prowl by its pale,
    mandrake hidden shrines.

These lightning-cloven marble walls, with sculp-
    tured images ornate,
Mark the imperial palace-walls where grand,
    gray-bearded kings held state.

Here were their soft and shaven lawns where
    fire-hearted tulips blazed;
Within these greenwood shaws the fawns up-
    on the fat grape-clusters grazed.

Here swans superbly floated by the barge
  moored to this marble stair,
Here shot a shining fountain high and foaming
  in the amber air.

Here, through these dim, wraith-haunted rooms
  swept many a noble courtier-train,
With velvets, diadems and plumes, the brave,
  the lovely and the vain.

And now we pass into the gloom of fragrant
  forests, and we see
The bright magnolia in bloom, the verdure of
  the banyan tree,

The lemon, green and golden-fruited, the cactus, with its crimson flowers,
The pied pinks, in the red-stone rooted, the
  hot, snake-haunted bamboo bowers,

The ring-dove rising while it sings, on whir-
  ring wings, till lost in light,
The rock-goat bleating while it springs from
  breezy height to breezy height.

And as we dreamily ride by between the ruins
  and the woods,
I think of blast and battle-cry that brake these
  baleful solitudes;

Of victories, forgotten now, defeats of which
  no wrecks remain,
Of laurel leaves on warriors' brows, of conquered
  leaders lying slain;

Of loves and hates. of joys and pains, of wel-
  comes and of fare-ye-wells,
Of sacrifices and of gains, of marriage-feasts
  and funeral bells.

I sadly sigh: Thus runs the doom—puissant
  kingdoms rise to fall—
The awful shadow of the tomb spreads wan
  and ghastly over all.

Then spake thee, O! thou friend of mine: All
  things of time shall be undone
Save Faith that makes our race divine and
  Eden-life and Earth-life one.

Since it hath lit its lamp upon the sacred shrine
  within my breast,
I feel that from my heart hath gone its phantom gloom, its vague unrest;

It seems that suns flood through the fierce and
  storm-jarred midnights wild with wrath,
That violets and daisies pierce the snows that
  drift upon my path.

When looking through the unclosed doors of
  charnel-vaults, I see afar
The sunny seas and shining shores beyond the
  coffin-worm and star;

When treading a deserted street where long-
  dead men and women trod,
I follow their white, spirit feet unto the very
  goal of God,

Where never thunder-bolt, and night, and
  pestilence, and battle-roar,
And wreck, and poverty, and blight, and age
  can harm then any more.

What matters it if we must lie at rest beneath
  the sea or sod?
Our spirits—though our bodies die—are rounding grandly back to God.

When in the white cathedral walls, where
    censer swings and cresset burns,
Where wave the purple funeral-palls gold-
    sprinkled o'er the gorgeous urns,

I hear the Mass, I am oppressed by the tear-
    broken, somber tones,
When *Passus et sepultus est* through the great,
    quivering organ groans;

But suddenly—the sorrow past—joyfully up
    my spirit springs,
When, like a silvery clarion-blast, clearly
    Et resurrexit rings!

Thus, in that land of wreck and wraith, I
    spake of vanity and loss—
When thou put forth thy purer faith I saw the
    crown above the cross!

I saw it—but I see to-day the sophistry behind
    it all;
From out the heavens, when we pray, there
    comes no answer to our call.

The very stones beneath our feet, the very stars
    within the sky,
Deny the Bible, and defeat its prophecies of
    By and by.

O, Soul, that has a hope of grace, and sees a
    glory-land afar,
That, with a rapt and radiant face, unfurls its
    white wings to a star!

O, Heart, so confident, serene and beautiful!
    I wish that I
Could see the palaces unseen that shine for
    thee beyond the sky;

But though it may not be, and though I feel
  thou art by Faith misled,
This one, vast, vital Truth I know, *Man cannot
die—there is no dead.*

Thee—not thy blood and flesh and bone—-but
  Thee—thy mind that makes the Thee—
Shall still unto Itself be known until the end-
less end shall be;

Shall revel in the dew, and ray, and bloom of
  every sun and sphere,
And pulse in every passing lay, melodious, that
  man shall hear;

Existence know in all that was, and is, and
  evermore will be,
And master immemorial laws, that now are infinite to Thee;

For man is God and God is man, whatever
  changes may befall:
To-day concentered in a span, to-morrow com-
prehending all.

HOPE

Comes she through the crimson mists of the
  morning strangely sweet,
There are flowers on her forehead, there are
  flowers at her feet;
Hers a trancèd look and tender, hers a rapt
  and radiant face,
And a perfect, pulsing poem is her grandly
  simple grace.

Now the sun-burst spills its splendor from the
    chalices of air,
And it shines upon her features and it sparkles
    in her hair,
And it flickers and it flashes on her white, up-
    lifted wings,
As she presses through the roses, while she
    rapturously sings,
While she strikes her sounding lyre with a
    siren touch and sings:

      If thou wilt follow me—
        Follow me where
          Shineth my palace-walls
      White in the air,
        All of thy dreams shall be
        Realized there.

      If thou hast eagerly
        Coveted fame,
          Laurels and lilies
    Shall circle thy name;
        Trumpets and tongues shall
        Thine honors proclaim!

      Youth, with the martial blood
        Hot in thy breast,
          Warrior plumes shall wave
    Bright on thy crest,
        And thy brave blade shall be
        Victory-blessed!

      Youth, with the thoughtful brow,
        Born to command,
          Badges and stars shalt thou
    Have at my hand,
        First in the councils and
        Courts of thy land!

Youth, with the piercing eye,
   Seeking the keys
      Unto the door of God's
Dark mysteries,
   Come, thou shalt baffle his
      Deathless decrees!

Youth, with the dreamy look,
   Strong and sublime
      Shall thy great tho'ts and grand
March down in rhyme
   Unto the uttermost
      Verges of time!

Youth, with the grasping hand,
   Thou shalt have gold
      And it shall buy for thee
Pleasures untold
   Until thine eyelids
      Forever shall fold!

Youth, with the loving soul,
   On thy true breast
      One heart shall seek there
Its raptures and rest,
   Faithfully blessing and
      Faithfully blest.   ˙

If thou wilt follow me—
   Follow me where
      Shineth my palace-walls
White in the air,
   All of thy dreams shall be
      Realized there.

Thus, with grand, gray eyes uplifted and with
      glory on her wings,
Presses she through purple roses, while she
   rapturously sings;

And we follow—on we follow, in a bright un-
broken train,
And with clear, uplifted voices join her brave,
triumphant strain.

    *   *   *   *   *

We are standing in the shadows of a twilight
wild and wan,
In a lonely land that never knew the dazzle of
a dawn—
In a land of ghostly ruins and of ghastly wrecks
that lie
Where a sullen river roareth underneath a sullen sky.
Where is now the singing siren who hath led
and lured us here
From the rest and from the rapture of contentment's charmèd sphere?
Over rocks and over rivers, through the passion and the pain,
Long we followed in her foot-prints, but we
followed her in vain.
By the wayside, spent and pallid, one by one
our comrades fell,
And we kissed their snowy foreheads while we
wept a fond farewell,
Leaving them to sleep the slumber of the
nameless and unknown,
In the immemorial shadow of the awful burial-
stone.
Still we followed her—and followed, till she
vanished from our sight,
Leaving us in desolation, on the dim edge of
the night.
Where are now her songs and garlands and
the gladness of her eyes?
Where are now the shining castles that we saw
within the skies?

Where are now the wreaths of glory, or the
    leal love, or the gold,
And the triumph of possession, and the thrills
    of which she told?
Vanished, like the flame and flowers of that
    magic morning-time
When she led and lured us hither with her
    prophecies sublime.
We are old and wan and wrinkled, grizzled is
    our golden hair,
In our eyes there is the hunger and the dumb
    look of despair,
And around us and about us gather in eternal
    glooms,
And before us and behind us is a wilderness
    of tombs.

        *   *   *   *   *

Hearken! through the storms and shadows
    one strong soul of souls sublime,
Speaketh: "Cheer ye up, my comrade, in the
    battle-march of time,
Self should be as less than nothing, for it
    perisheth as grass,
But the truths for which we labor from the
    world will never pass!
They will burst the chains of bondage—help
    the races to uprise,
And with Freedom's holy chrism will human-
    ity baptize!
Mourn not, comrade, for the selfish losses that
    thy life hath known,
Weep not for the gauds and baubles thou hadst
    hoped to call thine own;
Thine hath been a bright evangel—thou hast
    held a torch in air

Lighting on the struggling races from the
   realms of dumb despair;
Though thy very name shall perish when thy
   life is overpast,
Yet thy words and works forever through the
   centuries shall last.
Every good thought ever spoken, every grand
   deed ever done,
Is a fresh sword, making surer that our conquests will be won—
Conquest over Superstition, that hath ruled
   and ruined long,
Conquest of the captive peoples over mailed
   and mitered Wrong
In its palaces of splendor and its forts and
   bulwarks strong!"

"Glorious and gifted brother!" thus I sadly
   spake to him,
"Thine a spirit is that soareth o'er the narrow
   reach and rim
Of poor selfhood, and perceiveth what man's
   better aim should be,
But beyond these clouds and charnels my
   blind spirit cannot see.
I have borne so many crosses, worn so many
   chains, have passed
On from failure unto failure from the first unto
   the last;
I have known, my more than brother, O, so
   many burning wrongs!
Hate hath scourged me and hath scarred me
   with her scorpion whips and thongs.
By the men whom I befriended I have basely
   been belied,
By the land that I defended I have basely been
   denied,

Till my spirit, backward driven from the things
    it thought divine,
Cannot see in all the future a foreshadow or a
    sign
Of that white millennial morning when Human-
    ity shall be
God-like in the grand ideal thou hast pictured
    unto me.
Man will tear his fellow-mortal, suck the blood
    from out his heart—
For the old, old tiger-spirit of his very self is
    part—
He will trample on the helpless, spring the
    lock and forge the thrall
Till the final cataclysm our proud planet shall
    befall,"

"Nay, my comrade, man is better than he was
    in cycles past—
He will grow in grace and knowledge and in
    freedom to the last;
He will find the mystic Sangreal, tho' so long
    hath been his quest;
He will reach the heights resplendent—cast
    the beast from out his breast
And stand forth, in time, transfigured, beauti-
    ful, and bright, and bless'd!
Then, my comrade! O, my comrade, to our
    struggles and our strife
'Mid the thorns and burning plough-shares of
    our semi-savage life,
All his great and godlike freedom will he owe
    —as we to-day
Owe our semi-liberation from the Popes' and
    Princes' sway
To the Heretics and Rebels who revolted long
    ago

From oppression it hath never been our better
  lot to know!"

"Brother!   O, my more than brother!" and   I
  search his shining eyes,
Seeing all the look prophetic, luminant, that
  in them lies,
"With thine own pure inspiration I can see the
  golden goal
And can hear the songs victorious downward
  from the future roll.
For I know, O, more than brother! while upon
  our planet shine
Firm and dauntless, true and loving, and unselfish souls like thine,
They will light the races upward unto regions
  yet untrod,
Till on every human forehead shines the glory
  of a God!"

A DIAMOND DAY

It was a diamond day of my life—
  A day I will dream of through years to be;
It lifted me out of all storms and strife,
  For, Rowan, I was with thee.

I had rounded the world with its revels and
    spells
  Of every passion known unto man;
I had seen its heavens and felt its hells—
  For thus my destiny ran.

And love its glory and life its graces
  Had lost their power to cheer and charm,
And I envied the dead in their dwelling-places
  Afar from all hope or harm.

Then into my life and my love there came
  Thy presence, Rowan, and love and life
Were vivified with the vital flame,
  Immortal o'er storms and strife.

It sweetened and strengthened myself to feel
  The tenderful touch of thy thrillant palm:
It broadened and brightened my soul—thy
    leal
  Look—conquering and yet calm.

The garlands of glory are budding now
  That soon will blossom in bliss for thee
And a nimbus make for thy noble brow
  That the whole wide world will see.

Yes, thy victory yet will come, my own,
  With a blast of trumpets and roll of drums,
And a blaze of banners by winds outblown,
  And the cry: "He comes! He comes!"

And after thy triumphs and trials here,
  And the bays and blossoms that they will
    bring,
To a happier state and a higher sphere
  May thy sovereign spirit wing.

May the golden lilies of God, my own,
  Forever blossom around thy way
Afar in the fair and the fragrant zone—
  The zone of the Deathless Day.

FOUND

Our ship lay stilled within the calms
  Of seas confineless. Far away
  In the red southern distance lay
An isle with palaces and palms.
  Our wine and bread were well-near spent,
  And white and hungry sailors went
In knots apart. With bated breath
  They muttered things I could not hear,
  But still my heart was clutched with fear
Of nameless horrors and rude death.
  And days went by and we were cursed
  And crazed by hunger and by thirst,
  And then it was I knew the worst.
A mariner with whetted knife
Sprang up, and shrieked: "Draw lots for
    life!
Because one man of us must die
  That of his blood the rest may quaff,
That of his flesh the rest may eat—
O human flesh and blood are sweet,
The daintiest of draughts and meat!"
A maniac light was in his eye;
  A maniac tone was in his laugh;
And then I heard the sailors say,
"Yes! one of us must die this day!"
  They took the dice-box and they played,
  To see whose neck should feel the blade.
I shook it last, and, lo! the cry
Rang from all throats that I must die!
"Give me one hour, just one! " I plead.
  "That I may pray." They made consent:
  Prone to the hot, black deck I bent,

And asked that I might meet my dead,
Might meet my bride who sailed away
One sweet, bright morning in the May,
Who threw last kisses with her hand
To me upon the spumy sand,
Until the tall barque round the peaks
Of Cornwall disappeared, and I
Went with a sob that was a sigh,
With tears upon my boyish cheeks,
To wait for her return. But, no,
  She never did return to me,
  For tidings came from a far sea
That struck my heart as with a blow,
For the tall barque had sunken low
  Upon the hidden rocks. No more
  Would it sail homeward unto shore.
And as I prayed a cloud rose high
And blotted out the burning sky,
  And lightnings flashed from sky to sea
  As if the glory had got free
From out of heaven. Thunders rolled
With clash and boom, while uncontrolled
The winds sprang up and swept us on
  Unto the isle. We struck a rock—
  My senses left me with the shock,
And when I woke my strength was gone.
I staggered to my feet and, lo!
  I saw a land of light and bloom,
  A land of sunshine and perfume,
And all that nature can bestow—
With pleasant valleys. green and deep,
That mounted upward to the steep
  Of chalky cliffs, where curled the mist
  Of morning by the sunshine kissed
  To beryl, pearl and amethyst,
And all bold brilliance. Here and there
The palm tree tossed in amber air,

Up-springing in the gloom of green
Tall, shining sheaves of flowers were
    seen—
The reddest red, the bluest blue,
The whitest white—all dashed with dew,
All swaying on the supple stems
Of which they were the diadems;
And flaming birds that looked like flowers
    To which their God had given wing,
    That they might up and upward spring
Unto a whiter world than ours.
I walked the beach. The foamy waves
    Were chiming at my feet a tune
    That sounded like the subtle rune
Of some lost paradisic staves—
    When suddenly before my sight
    Stood up a city, vast and white,
With strange, majestic temple walls,
Deserted streets and voiceless halls,
    With dumb, proud idols, ruined shrines,
    Urns stained with sacrificial wines,
With stones for sacrificial rites,
And columns twined with parasites—
    All   blotched   with   bloody-calyxed
        blooms—
That led to still and solemn tombs,
Where funeral flags and fallen lamps
Were   streaked   with   somber   dust   and
        damps,
    And here and there in niches stood
    Brown mummies in the solitude,
Staring at me through sightless eyes
With looks of hideous surprise.
    And passing through the palace-door,
    Where kings had ruled in days of yore,
I wandered—spent and sore of heart,
    And sat me on the faded throne,

And wrung my hands, and made my moan.
When suddenly I heard the tone
And tinkle of a lute, the strands
Seemed quivering with quivering hands;
And then a sad voice sang, and I
Pressed down my heart, and thought to
    die—
For that same voice had sung to me
On a far shore beyond the sea—
Had sung to me, in mornings new,
In the June seasons when we walked
Through English meadow-lands, or
    talked
Where bloomed the cowslips dank with
    dew—
My bride—so tender and so true!
I sighed, "O, I am but asleep!
I dream! I shall awake to weep!
I dream!"— I said no more. For, lo!
I saw a vision in the gloom
And grandeur of that ancient room—
I saw a vision of my bride!
"O, blessed God!" I gladly cried,
"Her spirit I at least may see!
At least her spirit comes to me!"
And standing motionless I gazed
And gazed upon her matchless grace,
While like a radiant angel, dazed,
    Her soul-light flickered on my face.
Spell-bound, she looked within my eyes,
Then, with a sudden storm of cries,
    She fell upon my breast, and said,
    "Thou art not dead! thou art not dead!"
And thus the lost was found and thus
    From uttermost of continents,
    We were led back to love intense
By ways that were unknown to us—

By ways we never would have trod
Save through the guidance of a god.
Then, O, what joyous days we passed
Within that isle! How we went
Through bowers, swooning with their
    scent,
By blue waves where' green woods were
    glassed !
And talked of love until the stars
White-lidded hung within the blue.
And like a lyre through and through
    The night were heard the bulbul bars
Of melody. While in the gloom
Burned like a torch the cactus bloom,
    And all the land was lulled and dim
From purple rim to purple rim.

● WE TWO

No eyes like thine eyes can charm me, no
    voice like thy voice can cheer,
No clasp like thy clasp can thrill me, no dear
    one is half so dear;
Aye, dearer thou art, far dearer, than glory
    and place and gold,
And nearer thou art, far nearer, than ever on
    earth was told.

I may lose my faith forever in the heaven of
    which we hear,
I may learn to think it was nearest when thou,
    O, beloved! wert near;
I may lose my faith in the seraphs who sing
    by the jasper sea,

But, tenderest friend man ever had! I'll never
lose faith in thee!

I know not, my brother, I know not, if we
ever will meet again;
Dark and wild and uncertain are the devious
paths of men,
And far, O, far are we severed by mountain and
wold and waves,
And this is a land of partings and funeral-bells
and graves.

But whether we meet, or whether we meet in
this world no more,
I'll love thee still as I loved thee in the passionate years of yore;
The red blood will dance and tingle with pleasure throughout my frame,
And my heart will break into blossom whenever I hear thy name.

MYRA

O that August night!
O that August night!
The moon in the opal mid-air hung like a
wonderful blossom white!
As I dipped my oars in the diamond spray,
And our boat, like a sea-bird, flew away.
The beautiful Myra was with me there,
And the splendor of summer was in her hair;
The lilies of summer were in her face,
The soul of the summer was in her grace;
The song of the summer was in her tone,

The passion of summer was in her zone,
The glory that gladdens the summer skies
Was shining and soft in her blue, blue eyes.

O that magic night!
O that magic night!
The bridal of every beautiful dream and
blessèd that can delight!
The silver turrets and shining towers,
The hanging gardens of golden flowers,
The almond trees with their argent blooms,
By hoary temples and fanes and tombs,
The spicy scents from the shores outblown,
That tingled and thrilled through our blood
and bone,
And the songs of the bulbuls sung in time
With the wooing winds and the waves
a-rhyme,.
While over and under and through was blent
The mystical light of the firmament!

O, that passion night!
O, that passion night!
The palace-windows that fronted the waves
with torches were all alight;
And we heard the waltzers a-waltzing there,
And their laughter peals on the pulsing air,
While down through the glittering rooms
there went
The songs of the minnesingers, blent
With harps and bugles in strains divine
That fired our blood like the flame of wine!
And the stars were tangled within the spray
That dripped from my dipping oars away;
And my heart was tangled within the hair
Of the beautiful Myra before me there!

O, betrothal night!
O, betrothal night!
When God threw open his gates to us and led
    us into a land of light!
A land of love that was all our own,
And I was the king on a shining throne,
And Myra was queen, with an equal share
In all of the beauty that blossomed there—-
In all of the halcyon hopes and sweet
That threw their garlands before my feet—.
In all of the jubilant joys that came
With festal trumpets and flags a-flame—-
In all of my very self a part—
Spirit of spirit, and heart of heart!

O, God's own night!
O, God's own night!
That wafted Paradise down to us with all of
    its passionate delight!
The beautiful seasons have flowered and fled,
And sifted their snows on her shining head,
Since I told my love in our little boat,
While under the flower-white moon afloat;
But Myra is dearer by far to-night,
As she circles me close in her warm arms
    white,
Than even in passionate years long flown
When first I ungirdled her virgin zone;
And a tenderer beauty mine eyes can trace
Than they saw in her glorious girlhood grace;
And thus will our beautiful love increase
Till the infinite years of our souls shall cease.

A FRAGMENT

You may slobber of lovely girls,
  That thrill your heart with joy,
Of their beautiful eyes and their golden curls,
  And their manners soft and coy;
But of all the lassies on sea or land,
The one most charming and bright and grand
  Is the girl most like a boy.

THIRTY YEARS

O, the sun-dazzle that summer nooning—
  That summer nooning beside the sea!
The woods, a-tremble, were all a-crooning
  With trill of thrushes and boom of bee;
Danced the boats on the dancing billows
  Up and down in the crystal day,
Swung the birds in the swinging willows
  All a-sparkle with salty spray.
Over the vine-prankt mountain verges
  Tripped and tinkled a streamlet free,
Lost at last in the shaggy surges
  Out in the sand-dunes by the sea.
Over and over the free, fresh heather
  The beautiful butterflies waltzed away,
While Lily and I walked on together,
  Singing a rare, sweet roundelay;
Talking at times of the times thereafter,
  Merrily, O, so merrily we!

Breaking out into peals of laughter—
Laughter a-chime with the chiming sea.
On we walked through the warm, sweet
    weather—
Forest and foam were all a-tune;
On we went through the glad, green heather
And dreamed of the raptures a-coming soon—
A-coming soon with the bridal-kisses,
    Bridal-roses and bridal-ring,
And all the blessings and all the blisses
    That love—that passionate love could bring.
       *   *   *   *   *
"Farewell, Lily, I must be leaving,
    My ship is ready"—we parted there—
"I will return when the June is weaving
    Bridal-blossoms to wreathe thy hair."
Then I kissed her and I caressed her—
    Eyes a-shine with our unshed tears—
Then once more to my heart I pressed her,
    And we parted for—thirty years!
Yes; for my goodly ship went grinding
    Into the rocks one wrathful night—
Sheer through the surges black and blinding
    Sank the vessel and crew from sight;
I alone through the awful billows,
    Scarred and senseless was landward borne,
Waking, under the wet, lone willows
    Of a lost isle, with the morn.
       *   *   *   *   *
Come the summers with wreaths of roses,
    Come the winters with wreaths of snow—
Never a sail to my sight discloses
    Out on the rim of the sky-line low.
Thirty Junes with their thrills of passion,
    Thirty Junes with their throbs of pain,
Thirty Junes in the old, old fashion,

Live and perish and live again!
Came a ship to my lonely island—
Came a ship by the storm in-pressed—
Back they bore me again to my land
Under the under-skies a-West.

*   *   *   *   *

Up through the fisher-town I wander—
Never a passing face I know;
Many, ah! many are camping yonder
Under the sod of the kirkyard low.
Others have left for the alien-places,
    And, O! the lassies and lads of yore
Have lost the traces of youthful graces
That lit their faces in years before.
Out of the town to the lands outlying
    Over the blossomy gorse I go—
Flitter-birds through the air a-flying
    Sing as they flutter to and fro.
Who is that by the sand-dunes walking,
    Back and forth by the dunes of sand,
Watching the bright, brisk boats a-rocking
    Over the billows unto the land?
Poor, old woman! I hear her praying,
    Here—out here by the singing sea—
Heaven, O, heaven! What is she saying?—
    "Harold! my Harold, come back to me!
Thirty years I have watched and waited—
    My heart is sick and my heart is sore—
Where and, O! where art thou belated?
    Darling! my darling, come back once more!"
God! O God, it is Lily!

                                          Lily,
    I am thy Harold come back to thee."
Cruel her eyes and her accents chilly
    As slowly she turns her face to me:
"Thou my Harold? Ha-ha!" Her laughter

Breaks in a passionate flood of tears:
"Mock and madden me not thus after
Waiting and watching for thirty years."
"Lily, O, Lily! I am thy lover—
Why wilt thou mock and madden me?
See—thy locket. See—I uncover
Thy picture."

"Nay, it can never be;
Straight is Harold as any arrow,
Strong is he with the strength of youth"—
Cut her tones to my very marrow;
Slowly—slowly I saw the truth.
"Handsome is he with hair as golden
As yon sun-dazzle upon the bars,
With roses red on his cheeks unfolden
And eyes that shine like the summer stars.
Thou my Harold—Ha-ha!" Her laughter
Breaks in a passionate flood of tears.
Thus, O, thus do I meet her, after
Waiting and watching for thirty years!

A SUMMER PICTURE

The radiant summer-tide ringed our sweet star
With a girdle of glorified flowers,
And winds from the wonderlands fragrant and
far
Lent a tune to the tread of the hours.

The linnets sang loud and the linnets sang low
In the blossoming tops of the trees,
And the crimson-cupped tulips were bent to
and fro
By the madcap and merriful bees.

The heather was green on the low granite hills,
  And a silvery vapor was curled
Round the purple peaks, tinkling with turbu-
    lent rills
  On the uttermost edge of the world.

On the sands the white walls of a fisher-town
    shone,
  And the cross on its crazy old spire,
With ivy in infinite tangles o'ergrown,
  Was tipped at the topmost with fire.

The red-tiled farmsteads, moss-mantled and old,
  Rose out of their garden-plots gay,
And harvest-fields flashed in their glory of gold
  Through all of the diamond day.

A happy young lover rode dreamily by
  Through the depths of that tranceful retreat,
While cascades of sunshine poured out of the
    sky
  And blazed into bloom at his feet.

And Pauline, the pretty and passionate-eyed,
  With a heart that was tender and true,
In her gladful young gracefulness rode at his
    side
  Through the buttercups reeling with dew.

That day is long dead and that land lies afar
  Beyond the dark, billowy deep,
But the pale, golden gates in their dreams drop
    ajar
  And they see its old splendors in sleep.

THE DREAM OF A DREAM

The carking cares of life uplift—the passion
    and the pain;
The lamentation for a loss; the grasping after
    gain;
The memory of fickle friends who broke their
    faith with me;
The white rose blooming o'er the dead I never
    more may see;
The wrongs unspeakable that I have been com-
    pelled to bear;
The poison of the liar's tongue; the traitor's
    subtle snare;
All vanish, and my soul leaps up, triumphant,
    proud and free,
When the Poets—O the Poets!—sing their
    wild, sweet songs to me;
And breaking through my prison-bars, and
    scorning time and tide.
I live with old memorial things, I wander
    spaces wide.
Hot Afric jungles thick and green before my
    vision rise;
A cruel tiger crouches there with bright and
    burning eyes,
And in the shadow of a palm a naked native
    stands,
With lifted spear—the savage son of still more
    savage lands.
I see the desert stretching dim before mine
    aching eyes:
Oases with their plumy palms carved green
    against the skies.

And black Assyrian ruins where the tents of
    Arabs gleam;
And the solemn site of Tyre where the fisher
    dreams his dream;
And the stern and silent Pyramids, within
    whose ghostly gloom
The crowned and sceptered Pharaohs wait the
    trumpet and the doom;
And dim seraglios steeped in bloom my burn-
    ing senses see,
And minarets all crescent-crowned, when Poets
    sing to me.
I see a summer island in the heart of Indian
    seas,
Where the breath of reddest roses fills and
    thrills the throbbing breeze,   ·
As the shining shafts of sunset deepen in the
    Occident,
And the pallid moon's white splendor with
    departing day is blent.
Far above—the starry spaces of the purple
    tropic skies—
Far below—the landscape swooning in its
    bloom and beauty lies—
    And the *al sirat* seems swinging from the
    moon unto the shore,
And I almost see the angels, glad, victorious,
    trooping o'er.
Sweeter still the Bards are singing: In a grand
    cathedral's gloom
I am standing in the silence by an old Crusa-
    der's tomb—
Standing in the speechless silence, while from
    gilded pillars tall
Over lampless shrines the shadow of funereal
    banners fall.

But the organ's mournful music stirs the calm
    with muffled moan-
Swells into the trump of thunders—sinks into
    a tinkling tone —
Peals into a psalm of oceans—then the surg-
    ing music swoons,
And it is the silvery singing of the birds of
    spicy Junes.
But the vision breaks and changes. Louder
    now their songs upswell:
Of the glorious Grecian City of the Violet
    Crown they tell;
Of towers old and beautiful on Erin's saintly
    shore,
And of their hieroglyphics lost to legend and
    to lore;
Of Scotia, where of spear and shield within a
    hoary time
Blind Ossian struck his wizard harp and sang
    in strains sublime;
Of ancient Albion's castle-halls, where long
    ago her lords
Drank deep their horns of golden mead all at
    their wassail-boards.
I see the beetling Alps arise white with eternal
    snow
As when they rang with Gothic staves dim
    centuries ago:
I see Italia's gardens spread before mine eager
    eyes—
There splendor-shod the planets set and splen-
    dor-shod they rise:
I see Alaska's frozen heights, and Brunswick's
    forests dim:
The shores where sang the Puritans their
    wild deliverance hymn;

I see the thunder-cloven hills, the time-hewn
    canyons see,
As of the savage Occident the Poets sing to
    me.

    *   *   *   *   *

But now the shadow falls athwart the solemn
    sunset hills,
And dim the wild apocalypse that all this poem
    fills;
The winds are still, and with the hush a mist
    has settled down
Across the silent woods, across the white walls
    of the town;
No music breaks the silence; there is neither
    scent nor shine;
I lift mine eyes to the storm-sad skies—the
    dream of a dream was mine;
But the Poets—O, the Poets!—they will come
    to me again
When my heart is torn and bleeding on the
    Battle-field of Men.

THE MARTYR-BAND

When, looking through the mist of years, I
    hear the people's thunder-tones,
And see the glitter of their spears, the blessèd
    glare of burning thrones,
I worship Freedom's martyr-band in every
    atom of my soul,
Because through them our native land is free
    of Tyranny's control.

Upon the guillotine they shed their blood our
  fettered race to free;
They drank the draught of poison red; they
  died in chains for you and me;
And whether a Corday for France, an Emmet
  for old Erin's shore,
They helped Humanity's advance to heights it
  never scaled before.

Fragrant their memories to-day and flowering
  in the heart of man,
And theirs is the supremest sway that hath
  been since the world began:
The Truth they taught survives and shines in
  codes that are triumphant now—
Broad codes to which the august lines of auto-
  crats themselves must bow.

And, as the centuries increase, their influence
  to our star will bring
A time of universal peace that knoweth neither serf nor king,
Nor crime, nor chain, nor gallows-tree, nor
  poverty beneath the sun,
When one shall all the nations be and all flags
  blended into one!

SUNAMCAM

In the time—in the fair and the flowerful time
  Of the past—in the pride of our yearning
  and youth,
When life was a song, and the song was sub-
  · lime

10

With the spirit—the sovereign spirit- of
truth,

We met, and our meeting was more unto me
Than the crown of a Tsar, for thy friendship
was worth
All—all that the titles and treasures could be
Of the earth—of the whole wide and won-
derful earth.

We parted—we parted. Thy life was a leal
Devotion to duty—strong, tenderful, brave
And, O! if thy record my pen might reveal
Thy way would be glorified unto the grave.

We parted; yet through all my triumphs and
tears,
Thy friendship hath shone o'er my life like
a star;
Through the splendors and storms of the fugitive years
It hath followed me fondly and followed me
far.

And when in the sovereign reach of thy days
I heard that a leal love had come unto thee,
To hallow still further thy words and thy ways.
Through glories and glooms that we cannot
foresee,

My heart rose in rapture to feel that thy heart
A rapture divine had been destined to know,
To know—ere the mold and the miracle—part
Of the happiness heaven can only bestow.

May the rarest of lilies unfold for the eyes
Of thy radiant bride; may she hear—may she
hear

The sweetest of strains ringing down from the
    skies
Like an *Io triomphe,* brave, vivid and clear!

May sunbeams befriend her, and angels attend
    her,
Through day-tides that ever shall desolate
    be,
And all that is truest, and all that is tender
Their benisons bravest and brightest sur-
    render
To thine and to thee!

IMPROMPTU

I know a beautiful. blue-eyed boy,
Whose very name is a fount of joy
To all who have known his look and tone,
And the winsome ways that are all his
    own.

O! a brave, bright boy is this boy of mine!
How his red cheeks glow! How his grand
    eyes shine!
How merry his talk, and how graceful he!
How his laughter rings with unstudied
    glee!

Villadsen! May the roses bright
And radiant, with their dews bedight,
Stoop down all lowly and kiss thy feet
And make thy life with all joy complete.

I love thee! I love thee! and who shall dare
Deny me the right to this love declare?
Why, no one under the secret skies
That bar out the blisses of Paradise.

.

LOVE AND LUST

What is love? What is the subtle feeling that
    can blend a soul
With a fellow-soul forever, making of the twain
    a whole—   .

Making of the twain a mutual thought, con-
    viction and desire,
And a single ardent purpose unto which they
    both aspire?

Thus he questioned, looking skyward from his
    lattice, while afar
In the blue, immortal spaces shone a bright,
    immortal star.

Still a dull, red flame was burning in the west
    —the funeral light
Of the dead Day, passed forever into Nothing-
    ness and Night!

What is Love? Ah! dead Day lying where no
    life shall ever be,
Many a vow of love was spoken while thy soul
    was strong in thee—

Many a vow of love was broken in the circle of
    thy sun,
Many a fair and foolish woman in thy passing
    was undone.

Child of all the vast, vague cycles, knowing
   all they ever knew,
Yet thy lips were sealed and silent to the tenderful and true;

Knowing all the tears and treasons that from
   Love and Lust have sprung,
Yet thy lips were sealed and silent to the yearn-
   ing and the young.

Day, O, Day! my black soul beating at its bars
   accuses thee
Unto God within the glory of the scarlet sins
   of me—

Of the scarlet sins that sent her in her wild,
   pure beauty down,
And deserted her—a harlot—in the fierce heart
   of the town.

Hark! A voice comes ringing downward from
   a citadel afar
Through the still, immortal spaces, from that
   strange, immortal star:

Soul with fellow soul communing, free from
   all the rot and fire
Of the senses—proud, triumphant over every
   low desire;

Harmonized in every atom with the being on
   thy breast,
Throbbing with a perfect rapture, thrillant
   with a perfect rest;

Caring for no bliss supremer in the blossom-
   .   land above
Than the sanctity and splendor of her presence—this is Love.

And if Love the dead Day brought thee, it hath
    brought a sovereign thing,
And although a slave it found thee, it hath
    made of thee a king!

If it brought thee Lust, far better thine the
    grave-worm and the grave,
For although a king it found thee, it hath
    made of thee a slave.

If thy soul is pure as star-fire, and as proud as
    it was born,
It hath turned Lust from its portal with un-
    speakable, fierce scorn;

But if putrid, slimy, crawling, it hath turned
    sweet Love away
With a hiss and sting that slew her as the soul
    alone can slay.

Thou hast made thyself, and molded sense
    and soul, and thine the blame
For the scarlet sins that haunt thee and that
    daunt thee with their shame.

They will twine themselves as serpents 'round
    and 'round thy struggling soul—
They will strike and they will sting thee till
    the endless end shall toll!

Cowers he, and crieth hoarsely; "God! O. God!
    and shall it be?
Is there never a Nirvana where my spirit shall
    be free

"Of its consciousness forever?" * * * Silence
    in the solitudes,
Silence in the vast abysses where the awful
    secret broods;

Silence. Then a sharp cry shudders through the
    dewy dusk. Afar,
In the still immortal spaces, shines that strange,
    immortal star—

Shines upon his dead face lifted and his dead
    hands locked in prayer—
And the red moon lifts its crescent, and the
    roses scent the air.

THE MINNESINGER

The minnesinger struck the strings,
    And sang of sea, and sky, and sod
As but the types of mystic things
    Foreshadowed from the throne of God.

The flash of floods upon the sand,
    The sails and shadows on the sea,
The voice of forests, green and grand,
    The scent of lilies on the lea;

The snows of dark December hours,
    The violets of merry May,
The fronds of summer. and its flowers,
    The fall with golden fanyons gay:

The night, with purple deep on deep,
    Besprent with immemorial stars;
The fairies dancing on the steep
    Where fell the moonlight's yellow bars;

The shriek of winds, and woods, and
    waves,
    When storms were clanging in the sky,

The crash of throbbing thunder-staves,
  The flame of meteors hurtling by —

All these were fused within his strain,
  And lent a tongue to Nature, where
Before, mute, passionate, in vain,
  She yearned her secret sense to bare.

REGINALD VANE

The tulips were twinkling beside the still
    stream
Where we walked in the trance of a raptureful
    dream,
While through all the silence and moonlight
    and scent
Of the almonds, the song of the bulbul was
    blent.

        Reginald Vane!
        O, Reginald Vane!
I think of that hour with passionate pain,
For little I thought I would see thee no more
When the miracle joy of that moment was o'er.
The day broke in sky-fire, thunder and rain,
But I looked for thy coming and looked me
    in vain;
Then the dusk fell forever on me, and I knew
That thy love was a lie, and thine oath was
    untrue.

        Reginald Vane!
        O, Reginald Vane!
I would shield from thy soul the fell, terrible
    pain

That burned from my life all the beauty of youth
And belief in all purity, honor, and truth!
I cried to my pride, "Let the love that was leal
Be stamped in a transport of hate under heel!
Forget him forever!" But, ah! I would wake
To weep in the desolate dark for thy sake!

Reginald Vane!
O, Reginald Vane!
I knew that each tear on my soul was a stain;
But I could not—Christ, pity me—conquer the
spell
Of the past though it haunted and hissed me
to hell!

*   *   *   *   *   *   *

One night I sprang out of my sleep. Through
the bars
Of my lattice was sifting the light of the stars,
And there a dim, beautiful face I could see,
With an infinite tenderness turned unto me.

Reginald Vane!
O, Reginald Vane!
There flashed through my soul, and my heart,
and my brain,
The knowledge that out of thy palace of bone
And of blood thy false spirit forever had flown.

False spirit? Nay, nay! At the last—at the last,
When the idle illusions that led thee were past,
Thy spirit came back in its conquerless truth
To the one, fixed, unperishing love of its youth.

Reginald Vane!
O, Reginald Vane!
Thou art lying to-night under roses and rain;
But I know in the glorified gardens above
We will love through the consecrate cycles of
love!

PERCY

A terrible day rolled up in the east,
  And the sky was shot with a storm-red fire,
As the clamor of cannon and guns increased
  And the battle drums beat higher.

Then fell the night with a burst of rain,
  And lightning splintered the darkness vast,
While I pressed my face to the window pane
  Till the morning broke at last—

Broke in a wonderful flood of light
  That flushed the roses a redder hue,
And lent the lilies a whiter white,
  The pansies a bluer blue.

Clang! clang! the bells with rejoicing rang,
  And flags were from spire and ship un-
    furled,
While the masses their maddest Te Deum
    sang
  To the slaves of a waking world!

But, O! while many were mad with joy,
  I stood transfixed with a cruel pain
As they told to me how my blue-eyed boy
  In the front of the fight was slain.

What cared I then if my country's flag
  Should flash in triumph forevermore,
Or whether its dim, proud folds should drag
  The foeman fierce before?

I cared for nothing beneath the skies—
  All one to me was a crown or chain,
Since death had darkened my Percy's eyes
  On a far Virginian plain!

UNA

Una lay in her winding-sheet,
And candles burned at her head and feet.

Clarence came in his grand, young grace,
And looked with love on her fair, sweet
    face.

"O, Una! Una! my dream of bliss
Has turned to the dust of a burial kiss.

"I drank of lotus and dreamed that I
Saw beautiful virgins passing by.

"And they were fairer than seraphs are
Who wing and carol from star to star.

"But fairer than phantoms conjured up
By the potent spell of the purple cup

"Were thy beautiful face and form—but
    now
I must press a kiss on thy pallid brow,

And wander back, back to the world once
    more,
That never will be as it was before,

"And try to drown in the dreamy bowl
The sweetest memory of my soul!"

   *   *   *   *   *

Caryl came, and he knelt him there,
And he looked with love on her features
    fair.

"O, Una! Una! my heart is dead
And turned to dust in thy coffin-bed!
155

"O, darling! darling! I loved you so
That back to the world I can never go.

"I could not forget thee, O, my sweet!
I would not forget thee, were it meet.

"And yet the thought of thee lying low
Will mock and madden me—this I know!

"My heart went hungering through the
        world,   ·
But my look was cold and my lip was curled,

"Till into my life thy sweet love came
And set my spirit and sense a-flame.

"Immortal beauty illumed thy face,
O, fairest daughter of all our race!

"And the mystic strength of thy magic song
Had snapt the thrall and had staid the
        thong;

"But, O! thy beauty was naught to me,
Nor the magic spell of thy minstrelsy.

"I loved thee, sweet, for thy love alone
That blossomed in every look and tone.

"I stood in the light of thine eager eyes,
And saw a passionate paradise,

"And though my garments were stained
        with sin
Its gates were open to let me in.

"O, Una! Una! come back to me—
If I were dead I would come to thee—

"I would come to thee though the clods
        had prest

For a thousand years on my throbless
    breast!"

*   *   *   *   *

Part her beautiful eyelids now,
And the red blood mounts to her pallid
    brow;

Her white hands over her whiter breast
Stir with a sudden and strange unrest;

She rises out of her winding-sheet,
Radiant, flushing and strangely sweet:

"Caryl, never hath woman known
A truer love than is thine, mine own!

"In the thrall of my trance I heard them
    speak,
And I felt their tears on my cold, cold
    cheek,

"And I felt on my lips their kisses fall,
But I could not struggle, nor breathe, nor
    call,

"Till I felt the touch of thy tender lips
Thrilling my frame to my finger-tips;

"And heard thy passionate cry that came
To my frozen blood like a blast of flame;

"Then life leaped up in my heart's red core,
And the world rolled under my feet once
    more!"

*   *   *   *   *

The earth swept out of its brief eclipse
As he held her lips to his eager lips;

The morning-kiss on the world was prest
As he held her breast to his eager breast.

Then out of the marble halls they went,
Through gardens with golden lilies sprent;

And song and blossom and sun and bliss
Were blent in their first sweet bridal-kiss!

SONG OF THE TWENTIETH CENTURY

Hosanna! Lift up the bright palm-branches
   higher,   .
O, race that was ransomed through flood and
   through fire!
Ring, stormily ring! O, ye bells in the steeples!
Flash, merrily flash! O, ye flags of the peoples!
The monarchs have fallen! the people are free!
                    Vive, Liberty!

O! think of the time when the toilers were
   slaves
To the power of pitiless nabobs and knaves,
Who said they were specially set by the Lord
To rule with the rifle and scaffold and sword.

By a spurt of the pen or a wag of the jaw
They made vice a virtue, they made lust a law,
And often some infandous leman was known
To prompt the decrees that came down from
   the throne.

Unrestful and thoughtful the people became,
Aroused by oppression and plunder and shame,

And putting a Phrygian cap on a pole
They marched on their masters by saddle and
sole.

The thugs of the throne heard the thunder and
thrill
Of huzzahs and of hisses, proclaiming the will
And the wants of the mob, and they cowered
with fear,
For they felt the Twelfth Hour of Settlement
near.

The turbulent multitude, frenzied and fell,
They tried with their sweet, soothing speeches
to quell.
In vain! The storm, brewing through thousands
of years,
Brake in blood and in fire, in terrors and tears!

Sky-high were the temples of tyranny blown,
Knocked into a cocked hat were palace and
throne,
The king business stopped, and the folk of
that trade
Were turned out to labor with pen, loom and
spade.

Now is the Daybreak! Humanity reigns!
Gone are the gallows, the bastiles and chains!
Instead are the newspapers, suffrage and
schools,
And right is the might that our destiny rules.

Hosanna! Lift up the bright palm-branches
higher,
O, race that was ransomed through flood and
through fire!
Flash, merrily flash! O, ye flags of the peoples!
Ring, stormily ring! O, ye bells in the steeples!

The monarchs have fallen! The people are
free!
                                    Vive, Liberty!

MY VISION

The fire and flesh of my mortal being
    Slip from my spirit and, lo! I seem
Facing the whole vast universe—seeing,
    Feeling and knowing I do not dream.

Troop before me the grand, pure, glorious
    Friends who have filed through time and
        tomb
Into a sphere where they shine victorious
    Over the specters of Dust and Doom.

One beloved in my far, free boyhood
    Comes in his glad, bright grace once more,
Crowned with the crown of a perfect joy-
        hood,
    And kisses me as he kissed of yore.

"Comrade!" he cries, in his old, blithe fash-
        ion,
    Taking my hand in his old, fond way,
"Though I have passed through the pain and
        passion
    Of death I am deathless here to-day.

"Though in the grave is the garment mortal
    In which I was manifest unto thee,
Never in through that pale, chill portal
    Passed the part of me that is me.

"God is the glory that steeps with splendor
  The infinite universe through and through—
The love that is passionate, sweet and ten-
    der,
  And all that is noble and brave and true.

"The thought, the speech and the rapt desire,
  The miracle beauty of sea and sod,
The longings higher and ever higher,
  Are God—and we all are a part of God!

"Here is the Aiden, but Aiden is only
  The soul of the earth, of its evils free—
Not a sphere that is strange or lonely,
  Or far from the planet where mortals be.

"Here is our valley; the roses drifting
  In golden garlands from rock to rock—
The sun through the oleanders sifting
  Its beams on our old familiar walk—

"The walk that leads to the headlands older
  Fronting the vague, blue void of sea,
Where oft we talked in the twilight golden,
  And dreamed of the victor-days to be.

"Thus, O, comrade! the trysting-places
  And tender faces we knew in time,
Gladden us still with their spirit graces,
  When we have passed to this sphere sub-
    lime.

"Farewell!"—a flash of his wings uplifting,
  And, left once more on the mortal side,
I hear the desolate, lost winds drifting
  Over the prairies wild and wide,

And see the lights of the village burning
  Red through the sheeted mists, and see

The toilers home to their hearths returning,
And hateful and harsh is the world to me.

Hateful and harsh—but the rare, rapt vision
Has left a hope in my heart that I
Will live transfigured in lands elysian
With all that I love, in the by and by.

IS IT I?

Out of my slumber shines a vision
Of foamy forest and swirling sea;
A sweep of emerald plain elysian—
A flutter of white wings flashing free!

Sheaf on sheaf of the fairest flowers
Shiver and shine in the dripping dew,
And down through the deeps of the bud-
ding bowers
A glimmer of glad seas slipping through.

A tangle of songs and of sunbeams sifting
Out of the infinite inner skies;
A thrill of our unfledged wings uplifting
And reaching the raptures of Paradise.

There we stand in the warm June weather,
While woodlands quiver and wavelets
chime—
There we stand with our lips together.
And pulses rhyming a perfect rhyme.

God! Through the casement crawls the
morning—

The cold, gray morning—and where is
    she?
Seek where the amaranth is adorning
A grassy grave by a singing sea!

Shine the roses as in the olden
    Rapture-years when the world was young,
Sing the robins as in the golden
    Glory-years with a thrillant tongue;

Swings the world through the starry spaces
    Just as it swung when she and I
Saw the summer with all its graces
    And garlands beautiful file by.

But, O! for the passionate spirit missing
    Out of the waters and sky and wood!
And, O! for the clasp of her and the kiss-
    ing—
The joy unwhispered, but understood!

Lying low in my chamber lonely,
    Thinking of days that have drifted by,
Only one cry can I utter—only,
    "Heaven! O, heaven! and is it I?"

.

CLAUDE ST. CLAIRE

The lion of society was handsome Claude St.
    Claire,
Because his blood was blue, because he was a
    millionaire.
His *tusculum* in Chapel-street was a *recherche*
    place,

Set off with all that gold could buy, and all
    that culture grace.
The plate-glass windows shaded were by damask
    —which, withdrawn,
Revealed the terraces of flowers, the fountain
    on the lawn;
The matchless pictures on the walls, by master
    painters limned,
The lapse of crawling centuries of change had
    left undimmed.
There were statuettes from Florence: there
    were shells from far Kathay,
And relics from the ruins of dead cities, dust
    to-day:
There were gilded chairs and tables; there were
    shelves in cozy nooks,
Loaded with strange, monkish writings, and a
    motley wealth of books;
Rugs of tiger-skins, black-spotted, from the
    sultry Afric shores,
Lay upon the marble thresholds leading through
    the rosewood doors;
There were orange-trees whose verdure was be-
    powdered with the snow
Of the fragrant, flaky blossoms, bending
    down the branches low;
There were cacti, spiked and thorny, that with
    lamp-like luster bloomed,
And great, white, transparent lilies, by their
    golden hearts illumed;
There were passionate musk-roses, red as wine,
    as subtly sweet,
Rising up to kiss your forehead, falling down
    to kiss your feet;
From the many tripod vases trailed long ten-
    drils to the floor,
And their mesh of leaves was sprinkled with
    their flowers o'er and o'er.

* * * * *

In his dressing-gown and slippers lolling by
the fire there,
With the London *Times* before him, was the
haughty Claude St. Claire,
Smoking listlessly and reading, in a lazy sort
of way,
Of the doings and misdoings of society that
day,
When his lively little *valet* into the apartment
came
And with many a bow he ushered in a wan
and wrinkled dame.
"I am Lora Lisle," spake she, "prophetess of
things to be,
And appointed and anointed to decree thy doom
to thee!
Far over lands and over seas, through whirl-
winds and through flood,
Through midnight mists and noon-day heat
and battle-fields of blood,
Unto this city I have come, a purpose at my
heart,
And it shall be fulfilled, I swear, before I will
depart.
O Cora! O, my only one! my only thing to
love!
You charmed her from me as the snake in
jungle charms the dove.
She left my arms for yours. Alack! I saw her
nevermore,
Though I have searched from year to year and
searched from shore to shore;
And all this time men glance at her as at a
thing of shame,
While you, far guiltier than she, the world
does not defame.

'Your ways are ways of pleasantness, and all
    your paths are peace,'
While at my heart the gnawing worms of an-
    guish never cease."
"Hold! hold! you vixen," thus spake Claude
    with lips that looked a sneer,
"You know that it takes two to make a bargain
    —do you hear?
She was a party to the deed that has her ruin
    wrought,
A willing party—but this fact you seem to
    think as naught."
"Cease! devil! cease! Did you not vow to wed
    her at the time?
Think not with sophistries like these to hide
    or gloss your crime.
Speak not!" his tongue clave to his teeth.
    "Stir not!" he was bereft
Of motion—like a statue stood he there until
    she left.
"Now, hearken!" thus the sorceress: "Remorse,
    seize on your prey,
And haunt him in his dreams by night and
    in his walks by day;
A phantom at his hearth become, a specter at
    his feasts,
Till he shall shun the sight of man and min-
    gle with the beasts!
Desert him not, in youth or years, in sunshine
    or in shade!
Desert him not until he weds the woman he
    betrayed!"

* * * * *

She fixed a last, fierce look of hate on titled
    Claude St. Claire,
And then she left him—sweeping from the
    room with royal air.

*   *   *   *   *

He lifted up his face and wailed, then, staggering, fell prone
Upon the floor, a sight for man and angels to
bemoan.
He wrung his hands, he clutched his heart, he
shrieked in his despair,
Until his *valet* hurried in to find him writhing
there,
And moaning: "O my God! my God! have pity
upon me;
Now in its scarletness that sin for the first
time I see.
Forgive it! O, forgive it!" but in vain, in vain
the cry—
It seemed to fall back on him and to crush
him from the sky.
He felt that his false, faithless soul would still
be crucified
Until he sacrificed his place, his family, his
pride.
"It cannot be! it shall not be!" cried lofty
Claude St. Claire,
"I will defy remorse!" he hissed, "I will defy
despair!"
And plunging into pleasures he had shunned
with scorn till then,
He soon became a favorite with all the fast
young men—
Became a hanger-on of clubs and green-rooms;
lower still,
Descending rounds of vice he went his time
and thoughts to kill.

*   *   *   *   *

The heads of idle exquisites were turned with
his success,

They envied him his intrigues, and they copied
    him in dress,
And a "lucky dog" they dubbed him—seeing
    not behind the veil,
Knowing not his tribulations, hearing not his
    smothered wail;
Knowing not the while he jested, with a smile
    upon his lips,
That his heart was racked and bleeding, and
    his soul was in eclipse;
Knowing not the while he reveled in debauch-
    ery that he
Saw a skeleton beside him that none other
    eyes might see.
In his restless dreams and frantic flew he from
    an unseen wrath,
Through a vast, unending forest, down a dark,
    unending path,
Where from black, unsightly marshes did a
    deadly vapor rise,
Sickly, yellow and polluting to the black, tem-
    pestuous skies;
Lurid lightnings shot and flickered through
    the thick, portentous gloom,
And was heard the rolling thunder, boom re-
    plying unto boom;
There long, prickly vines were rankly dangling
    down from bough to bough,
And they tangled in his tresses, and they stung
    and smote his brow;
There the bats wheeled in a circle, there the
    green snake, glittering, sprang
From its hideous coil before him with a viru-
    lent, sharp fang.
Strange, unshapely pagan idols, standing here
    and there he saw,
Staring through the weeds upon him with a
    still, majestic awe.

Dim, uncertain ghosts were flitting through
the solitude, the while
That uncanny voices muttered things all blas-
phemous and vile.
Waking to the lash of conscience, he would
gnash his teeth and rave
For the rapture of destruction, and the shelter
of the grave;
Till at last, worn down and nervous, he was
all too weak to play,
In the *salon* or the brothel, part of gallant light
and gay.
He became a very hermit—living far withdrawn from men,
With the brutes for his companions, in a green
and peaceful glen.
But in flying self no mortal has succeeded
through all time—
For within us, not without us, is the dreadest
doom of crime.
Thus it was with Claude—his lonely and se-
cluded hermit-cell
In the hushed and sunny woodland was to him
a very hell;
And the glimpses through the greenwood of the
sky, serene and blue,
And the lush of vernal branches, and the wild-
buds dripping dew,
Seemed to his phrenetic fancy blurred by baleful smoke that rose,
With a hot and palsied motion, from the flaming world of woes;
And the twitter of the song-bird and the chiming of the wave
Seemed to mingle with the ravings of the
damned beyond the grave;
Till at last his pride was humbled—pride of a
fierce, kingly race,

That through centuries had trampled on the
    poor and weak and base.
"O, thou devil, thou hast triumphed!" with a
    fearful curse he cried,
"I must bow unto thy bidding—Cora shall be-
    come my bride;
But hate rankles in my bosom, and I swear
    that I will mete
Out revenge unto the demon who thus brings
    me to her feet."

      *   *   *   *   *

So he wandered from the woodland back unto
    the world again,
And straight went he, without staying, to a
    gilded bawdy-den.

      *   *   *   *   *

There he found his Cora, dancing with a *roué*,
    in a room
Bright with gas and gay with music, perfumed
    by the tropic-bloom;
Heard he many a lustful whisper, heard the
    full wine-glasses clink,
Saw the wrecked but lovely women toasts unto
    their lovers drink.
"Cora," spake he softly, "Cora, leave, O, leave
    this shameless life
And I will forgive thy sinning, and thou shalt
    become my wife."
"*Dost thou dare!*" she started from him, and
    she stood before him, there,
In her trailing amber velvet, and the jewels in
    her hair.
Fair her face, but cold and cruel, lit by eyes
    whose eldritch flame
Hungry, changing, darting, restless, told of
    sin and told of shame;

Golden, silky tresses twisted into many a curl
  and braid
On her rouged and powdered features threw a
  ripe and tawny shade,
And her thin, red lips were parted with a proud
  and scornful look,
While her form, imperious, queenly, with her
  very fury shook,
As she spake: "Once—once, thou traitor! I—
  I would have been to thee
More, far more than any woman in this world
  will ever be;
For I worshiped thee to madness, aye, to very
  madness, man!
As the sun himself is worshiped by the priests
  of Ispahan;
How, O! how did you repay me? Dragged me
  to my ruin down,
Then deserted me, a harlot, in the cold streets
  of the town!
Fiend, however sunk in vices, dark, repulsive,
  I may be,
In the sight of the Impartial I am purer far
  than thee.
Aye, thou art as far beneath me—*me*, a lost and
  guilty thing—
As Apollyon in the fire, to Ithuriel on the
  wing!
Go! thy presence is pollution! Go!"—she proud-
  ly turned from him,
While he, livid with his terror, shivering in
  every limb,
Choked and reeled, then blindly, deafly,
  madly, rushed he to the door,
Sped into the rain and darkness, and was
  seen of man no more!

ANONYMA

The sunlight is slanting through woodlands uplifting
Their merry green garlands beside the blue
sea,
The songs of the happy young reapers are
drifting
Far over the harvest-fields hither to me.

Once in a miracle-morning together
This landscape was limned in our eager
young eyes,
While over the far cliffs all fringy with heather
We saw a white sail blossom out of the skies.

It bore to our beautiful manse a bright stranger,
As handsome as any young god on a throne,
And, fool that I was! I was dreamless of dan-
ger,
Believing your blameless, white heart was
my own.

Did I reproach you, O, wonderful woman!
When you surrendered your soul to his lust?
Never! For knowing your passions were human
I threw you a rose where you lay in the dust.

Forever from trust and from tenderness parted,
A proud and a passionless cynic to be,
I threw you a rose I had kissed, and departed
Again to a world that was worthless to me.

Did I reproach you, O, wonderful woman!
Sweeter by far than the sweetheart of God!

Nay, for I knew that your passions, though
    human.
Had nothing in common with me, a poor
    clod.

Then bless you, my bride! Though your sins
    are as scarlet,
They whiten as wool in the light of my love;
And though you are living the life of a harlot,
I place you the purified angels above'

OPTIMISM

The juice which this jasper cup contains
Was pressed from a poppy of Persian plains—
A poppy changed by a subtle power
From an ugly seed to a lovely flower—
A flower that caught in its crimson snare
An occult influence from the air.
To charm the sense. and the soul to cheer,
And render the riddles of life more clear.

I will drink the draught, for my heart beats
    low
With the weight of its weary, unwhispered woe;
For once in the passionate years of old
I loved a friend with a love untold;
But I thought him false, for I thought that he
Had lured the heart of my bride from me;
So I threw my glove in his grave, sweet face,
And ,we met in a moon-lit forest-place.
Our bright, keen swords from their scabbards
    sprang
And flew together with clash and clang,

But his brittle blade in the battle broke,
And I drave him down with a swift,sharp stroke.

A cloud passed over the pallid moon—
A witch-whelp barked in the black lagoon—
A shuddering wind the branches blew,
And a raven croaked as it downward flew.

Suddenly Carolyn spake to me:
"My friend, I never was false to thee,
But God forgive me my sins below
As I forgive thee this fatal blow.
The heart of thy bride is of blemish free,
She is my sister, and true to thee."

"Thy sister?" I shrieked, "thy sister? No!
Say to me—say that it is not so!"
Thus, with a pitiful cry, I plead,
Kissing and kissing the dumb, white dead,
Pushing the gory and golden hair
Back from his forehead so broad and fair,
When a resonant cry rang in my ear,
And I staggered back with a nameless fear,
And there in that lonely forest-place
I stood with my young bride face to face,
With the corpse between us! She lifted high
Her slim, white hand to the stormy sky,
And there by her dead, by her murdered dead,
She called for a curse upon my head.
And then she fell on the scarlet sod
And yielded her white ghost unto God.

I drink of the draught this cup contains,
Its fire flows through my frozen veins.
Wing-footed I walk in a lovely land
By skies of violet splendor spanned;
I pause in a pleasaunce, and I behold
A pearly palace with gates of gold,
Lapped in a glorified garden, where

The fountains flash in the amber air.
From fluted vases as white as snow
The fire-cupped flowers flame and flow;
The scintillant sunlight drips and drops
Through plumy palms and through citron
    copse;
The song-birds sing in the swinging spray
Then flit, like a flight of stars, away
To the lambent lake where the lotus laves
Its purple petals within the waves.

But, look! for my sweet bride I behold,
And the friend I loved with a love untold!
They come to me and they clasp my palms—
Their touch my turbulent spirit calms—
And thus my Carolyn comforts me:
"It is best that whatever is should be.
The hidden plan of the Universe
Is perfect. Never a crime nor curse
But had its mission, and it will be
Unveiled to our eyes in Eternity."

Softly and sweetly breathes my bride:
"Forget the desolate night I died,
Forget the blood that was blindly shed,
Forget the withering words I said.
Fate foreordained that thy hand should smite
My darling brother that dreadful night.
Then be courageous and be content,
Thou art innocent—thou art innocent!"

The vision vanishes—but a blest,
New hope is nestling within my breast,
And over and over it says to me:
"Whatever is, it is best should be."

LAUNCELOT

Here in my lone, lampless chamber I stand
  Close by the casement, and look through the
    pane
At the wild, roaring sea rolling up on the sand,
  Where the lights of the village shine red
    through the rain.

Shiver the roses that drape the gray eaves.
  'Reft of their glorified garlands of bloom,
While in the kirkyard the wan, ghostly leaves
  Flutter and fall over temple and tomb.

Many and many Octobers ago,
  Afar in the dust of a desolate year,
We parted in passion where shrubs cowered
    low
  And the hiss of the serpent was heard in the
    wier.

The sickly moon turned into blood as I wept,
  And the pale stars went staggering under the
    clouds,
When, lo! from the graves where thy ancestors
    slept,
  Came shuddering skeletons out of their
    shrouds!

They pointed their terrible fingers at me:
  "Curse thee, and curse thee!" they all spake
    as one—
"He had delivered our house but for thee,
  Now we are ever and ever undone!"

The brave suns have risen, the brave suns have
    set,

And dim are my blue eyes and bonny to-
  day,
And fairer than fleece are my tresses of jet,
  And the wrinkles have driven the roses
  away;

But still this bright thought brings an infinite
  calm:
  I will meet with my lover all tender and
  true,
When unto the Isles of the Lyre and Palm
  I set my white sails and go journeying, too.

But out of the dust of that desolate year
  Rings the curse that is written in blood on
  my brow,
And my heart is crushed down with a desperate
  fear —
  Launcelot, Launcelot, where are you now?
  O, where are you now?

ETERNITY ON EARTH

                          "That face!
I turned and fled from the moonlit place—
Turned with a quivering cry and fled,
For the grave had surrendered its dear, sweet
  dead!
Back in my unlit room, I drew
The curtain; the vines were dripping dew,
And flashed in the moonlight, keen and cold,
As they flashed in that nameless night of old."

"My darling, you dream!"
　　　　　"O, mother mine!
I was standing there, where the trumpet-vine
Drips fragrance over the rocks below,
When I heard a voice that I used to know—
When I saw a face I had seen before—
A face that will haunt me forevermore;
For, O! on a nameless night like this,
While Time was reeling through bloom and
　　　bliss,
And Christ was reaching our world to kiss,
I met him there where the trumpet-vine
　　Spills fragrance over the rocks below,
And he said that his rapturous love divine
　　I never and never again should know;
My blood was turned into madding wine,
　　And I killed him there, for I loved him so,
And the sea swirled up, and the crimson sign
　　Was washed from the shivering sands—
　　　but, O,
Its stain is forever upon my soul,
Till the funeral-bells for Christ shall toll!
Till the funeral-bells—O, heaven, forbear!
He is standing there! He is standing there!"

"What! on the lawn?" spake the Lady Lisle,
　"Why, that is Sir Sidney.   Come with me.
You never have met him; a little while
　Ago he came from the Afric sea."

They passed through the palace-halls,
　They met Sir Sidney, the soldier who knew
　　· no fear—
In tones that ring down the cycles yet,
　He cried: "Thou traitress, and art thou
　　here?
My blood is upon thy hands!"

And then,
He said, with a start and a silly smile,
"I was dreaming a strange, mad dream again—
Forgive and forget it, my Lady Lisle."

    *   *   *   *   *

And she who killed him, in the life before this
    life, became his own,
And happier were they, I hold, than God upon
    his golden throne!

    *   *   *   *   *

The men who walk our streets to-day will walk
    them when a thousand years
Have drained their flesh and blood to dust and
    blown it to the furthest spheres.
And I will meet thee yet, my love, within a
    forest still unsown,
Or city still unbuilt, and I will kiss thy scar-
    let lips with mine;
And though thy alien grave to-day by August
    grass is overgrown,
I know that thou art living yet in zone of
    palm or zone of pine—
Art living in a skeleton and skull and skin, to
    me unknown,
But in the cycle unconceived thy soul and
    body will be mine;
For thou wilt die and live and die a million
    times, mayhap, until
The atoms of the universe shall readjust
    themselves once more—
Just as they were when first we throbbed with
    the unwhisperable, hot thrill,
While palpitating breast to breast within the
    morning-years of yore!

IN A MAD-HOUSE

Come back, come back to me for an hour,
   And speak to me, sweet, as you spake of old!
Wear in your ringlets the red, rank flower
   I tore from the grass in the graveyard mold—
I tore from the grass where the dead boy sleeps
   With the worms, in his windowless palace
      low;
Where the trail of his brave, bright blood still
      creeps
   As it crept in the starlight long ago.

The devilish roses kissed my face
   And my hair was dripping with starry dew,
When I met him there in our trysting-place
   And killed him, sweet, for my love of you!
The universe gasped like a thing in pain,
   The moonbeams struck at the shrieking sea,
The sod lay shuddering with the stain
   And the golden lilies shrank back from me;
But my heart sang high as I went my way
   With a hiss of hate for the blameless boy,
Then limb to limb by your side I lay
   And throbbed with a thrill of God's own joy,
For you slept in my bare, blest arms—but, O!
   They bore me off to this prison-place,
And suns of splendor and swirls of snow
   Have drifted by since I kissed your face!

Then come. O! beautiful demon! Come!
   In a few swift, fugitive years at best
You and I will be lying dumb
   And blind to all that our love possessed;

But I will hunt you and haunt you there
    From zone to zone through the fields of fire,
And I will rivet the chains you wear,
    And I will baffle your last desire.
If Christ shall summon you to his spheres
    I will smite you back as you seek to soar,
And flames of Hades shall dry our tears
    And melt us together forevermore!

Then come, O, come to me for an hour,
    And speak to me, love, as you spake of old!
Wear in your ringlets the red, rank flower
    I tore from the grass in the graveyard mold—
I tore from the grass where the bright boy
        sleeps
    With the worms, in his windowless palace
        low;
Where the trail of his beautiful blood still
        creeps
    As it crept in the moonlight long ago!

THE POET-BOY

In memory of John W. Robb, Jr., Rosedale, Miss.

The bright June-lights were shining, like the
    gladdest smile of God,
The white June-lilies sparkled in the fresh and
    fragrant sod,
The sweet June-winds were winging through
    the flowerful woods and fair,

The wild June-birds were singing in the vivid
    arc of air;

Never did a morn diviner on our roseful Sunland rise,
Since the glad stars sang together in the blue,
triumphant skies!

Then it was, O, Poet-brother! then it was I
saw thee last!—
There the lights concenter on thee in my King-
dom of the Past!
How the jocund hours went dancing! and what
friends we met that day!
There was Holland, the great-hearted, who
has gone the heavenly way;
There was Falconer, the fearless,—wept with
O, such wistful tears,
And Frank Walter in the brightest flush and
splendor of his years!

In a glorious procession, with the gifted and
the brave,
With the beautiful and loving, they have filed
through the grave
To the star-spheres sempiternal, far beyond the
secret skies,
There to walk beside still waters, under palms
of Paradise!—
There to dwell with highest heroes who have
lived and died for man
Since that far, fresh-hearted morning when
humanity began.

And while still our tears were falling where
their shining foot-prints be,
Suddenly there came a summons, and this time
it came for thee.
In the sweet and stainless splendor of a life
and love supreme
Thou must pass the star-lit portal to the Realm
of which we dream;

Thou must leave thy ringing lyre, wreathed with
  half-blown flowers, unstrung,
Leave thy labors uncompleted, and thy sweetest
  songs unsung.
Why was it? O, why was it? In vain—in vain
  we cry—
From out the far, white citadel returneth no
  reply.

*   *   *   *   *

The day when last we spake farewell is dead
  forevermore,—
No summer in the years to be its radiance can
  restore.
As bright the skies may shine, as white the
  flaky lilies flower,
The winds may wing, the song-birds sing, as
  in that halcyon hour,
But, O, its occult loveliness, its subtle thrills
  of bliss,
Its mystic lights and melody forever I will miss,
For thy presence, O, thy presence, there I
  nevermore will see,
And with thee from the vision went its very
  soul from me.

But there is a Revelation, and it redes itself
  to man—
Known it was in every cycle, unto every creed
  and clan,
Taught the simple heart primeval by the still,
  small voice within,
Prompting it to deeds of duty—urging it to
  shrink from sin,
Pictured on the cliffs and lowlands, chiming in
  the surge of seas,
Glowing in the star-dust golden, blossoming in
  shrubs and trees,

Beaming in the looks love-lighted of the tender and the true,
Whispered by the lips of spirits sheltered from
our mortal view,
Speaking in our hopes and yearnings, and our
dim dreams of the night,
Tempering our tears and passion when a twin-
soul takes its flight,
Proving stronger and supremer as the world
heaves high and higher
From the depths of superstition and the mists
of low desire!
And this Revelation redeth that our dead have
never died—
That it was the yoke and fetters only that they
laid aside,
That they live in Kingdom fairer than is lit by
mortal sun—
Thrilled with triumph at the conquest and the
crown forever won—
Live where purer joys and purer draw them to
diviner plains,
And forever, reaching toward them, some new
happiness remains,
Where with victor-songs of gladness they will
welcome us at last,
When the fitful frost and fever of our lives are
overpast.

And I know in that leal Kingdom is thy lyre
heard to-day,
Sweeter, sweeter and completer than when
manacled with clay—
For I know thy spirit liveth, and I know it
leadeth still;
That a high and holy mission it will help us
to fulfill.

Though we strew the rose and lily on thy
  youthful shrine with tears,
There is this to recompense us, that through
  all the rounding years
Thou wilt lead us high and higher to the
  bright, victorious spheres!

  *   *   *   *   *

Poet-brother! Poet-brother! when the white
  magnolias bloom,
Or the wintry yews are weeping at the dark
  door of my tomb,
In the Country of Contentment may my friends
  and comrades be,
Poet-brother! _ Poet-brother! thee, and great,
  grand souls like thee!

NEW YEAR

Out of the future, dumb and dim,
  The New Year comes to-day,
And a rollicking world is receiving him
  In its old memorial way.

With feast and frolic in hut and hall,
  And many a cheer and chime,
And the "Happy New Year unto ye all!"
  That comes from the olden time.

What will he bring to you, my friends,
  What will he bring to me,
Before his last dark hour descends
  In a midnight yet to be?

Life will he bring unto babes unborn,
  With its miracle moods, we know;
Some to splendor and some to scorn,
  Through all of their lot below;

Death will he bring unto many, and dear,
  Brave hearts will beat their last
Before the chimes of the next New Year
  Shall tingle upon the blast;

Tears to many who smile to-day,
  Smiles to the tearful ones,
In the same old merry or mocking way,
  For thus our destiny runs.

Bridal blisses to many a soul,
  Burial shrouds to more;
For thus are blended delight and dole
  Till all of the years are o'er;

Yet, hail ye the New Year, bonny and
      bright,
  And hope that his sovereign hands
Will scatter liberty, love and light,
  All over these lower lands;

And whether he favor or fell thee, boys,
  In the battle and blare of Time,
Strike gallantly out for the golden joys
  And the higher heights sublime.

PROGRESS OF THE PEOPLES

Upward, upward press the peoples to that
    pure, exalted plane,
Where no throne shall cast a shadow and no
    slave shall wear a chain.

They have trampled on the fagots—broken
    crucifix and wheel,
Banished block, and thong, and hemlock, and
    the headsman's bloody steel;

Forced the Church-hold to surrender stake, and
    scourge, and bolt, and bar—
Torn the keys from off its girdle—thrown the
    gates of Truth ajar;

They have forced the titled tyrants human
    rights to recognize,
And with bayonet and saber they have slain a
    legion lies;

They are lighting lamps of freedom on a mill-
    ion altar-stones,
With the torches they have kindled at the blaze
    of burning thrones;

And this light will sweep and circle to the
    very ends of earth,
Touching with immortal beauty every heart
    and every hearth—

Thrilling every human being underneath the
    silent skies,
And transfiguring our planet to a perfect par-
    adise!

187

As we higher march and higher on   into this
    light serene,
Every man will be a kaiser, every woman be a
    queen—

Ay! queen-regnant, then, and ransomed from
    the thralls she wears to-day,
While her husband, son and brother, walk un-
    fettered on their way.

She hath wept and prayed in passion—bitterly
    hath made her moan—
All the terrors and the tortures of the tyrants
    she hath known—
Still, the blood that flows for freedom flows
    for man, and man alone.

Nay, behold! the light is burning with a strong
    and stronger flame,
And the foremost in the phalanx see the stark
    and stinging shame—

See the biting, blasting, burning shame of sex-
    oppression now,
And, with hearts and hands uplifted, swear a
    grand and godlike vow,

That, despite the fangs of Custom and despite
    the Church's frown,
Womanhood shall wield its scepter, womanhood
    shall wear its crown.

She hath borne with man his crosses, she hath
    worn with man his chains;
She hath suffered all his losses, she hath
    suffered all his pains—
She shall stand with him, co-equal, on the
    pure, exalted planes!

BETRAYED

"Room for the hero! Room!"
  And the mob fell back at the cry,
As under the flags and over the flowers
  A pageant proud swept by—
To the roar of cannon and ripple of trumps
  A pageant proud swept by.

A girl—a girl of the pave—
  Was all I could claim to be;
The soul of my sweet, pure, virgin self
  Had been betrayed from me
By a devil who looked like a god divine—
  Had been betrayed from me.

"Now, who is this hero—who?"
  I thought in a languid way,
And pressed through the clamoring crowd
      to see
  Its demi-god of the day—
The warrior, king or statesman who
  Was its demi-god of the day.

O, Christ! It was Carolyn,
  Who had ruined and wrecked my life
By his vow—by his false and his fatal vow
  That I should be his wife—
His vow that had dragged me down to hell
  That I should be his wife.

A puff of smoke, a flash,
  A whistling ball, and he
Lay dead all under his horse's hoofs,

And damned through the life to be—
Lay dead in his veriest victor hour,
And damned through the life to be

Then, O, how the rabble raved!
How it tore me with tooth and fang!
And I was borne to this dungeon dark
    While the air with their curses rang—
While the air of that soft, bright Paris
    morn   .
With their pitiless curses rang.

They will drag me out to-day
    To the guillotine, and my head
Will drop in the basket as my blood
    Stains it a fiercer red—
Stains France—stains all of humanity
    A still more savage red.

But I hold this sovereign truth
    That my act was right—was right!
He had taken my better self from me
    And hurled it down to night—
Had taken the life of my soul from me
    And hurled it down to night.

VICTOR

"Victor, my Victor!" Out of my sleep I sprang
    as I spake thy name,
For, O! I had seen thee in a dream—had
    looked in thy bright, brown eyes,
And thy laughter and look, and thy tone and
    touch were the same—were the very same

As of old when this passionate planet of
    ours to us was a paradise.

"I was only dreaming," I said to myself, and
    I gazed from the lattice where
The golden moonlight was sifting through
    the boughs of a blasted tree,
And I saw—I saw with a shudder and sob a
    gray old gravestone there
That bore the name of a noble one who was
    body and soul of me.

"Victor, O, Victor!" I cried once more, when
    thy sovereign hour was near.
And I clasped and kissed thee, O, comrade
    mine, with a mad, fierce, hopeless moan.
I heard thee whisper, "Be brave, O, heart!
    though unto an unknown sphere
My soul is passing, I will come back unto
    thee—my own! my own!"

Then through the oriel windows stole a ra
    diance half divine,
And a zephyr wafted the rose-leaves in from
    the garden green outside,
As Samæl set upon thy brow his awful and
    august sign,
And they said that between us lay at last a
    universe waste and wide.

But I spake, with a smile of scorn for death,
    "My darling will come to me!
Though his atoms shall blossom again with
    life in the pure, sweet pansy flowers,
Though they drift with the clouds in the crys-
    tal sky over many a dim blue sea,
Or trill in the throats of the singing-birds as
    they swing in the budding bowers;

"Ay! though they glitter in grain-fields bright,
 and, passing from form to form,
They enter the bodies of other men, and on
 through an endless chain,
I know—I know he will come to me with his
 passion sweet and warm,
And wonderful as it was of yore, without one
 spot or stain!"

But, Victor, Victor! thy vow is still unvital-
 ized by thee.
Though our planet has passed through the
 suns and snows, the songs and the sobs
 of years;
And my soul in agony has appealed to gods
 that it cannot see
Till, ground into unbelief at last, it breaks
 into bloody tears.

    *   *   *   *   *

God! what is that by thy gravestone there—
 that strange, ineffable light
Instinct with the life that throbs in me—it
 seems of myself a part.
What subtle essence has entered earth and uni·
 verse and the night?
And what is it calling unto my brain and
 spirit and sense and heart?

Victor, O, Victor! it is thee! I feel it is thee,
 my own!
No longer a solitary self, but blent with the
 universe,
Thrilled through with every blessing it knows
 or has ever known,
Yet bearing with pure, brave, marvelous
 power its every crime and curse;

A part of all that has ever been, is, or will ever
be,
From the yellow light of the planet to the
yellow primrose there;
A part of the very Godhead, and the glorious
part of me;
A part of the crawling serpent, and a part of
the bird in air!

And I know when out of the finite to the infinite I shall go,
I will shine in the light immortal of the sun
upon my grave,
I will bloom in the red, proud roses that out
of my breast shall grow.
And live in the larger freedom of the wind
and wood and wave.

I will laugh in the little children; I will love
in the lover's breast;
I will cry with a vast, keen rapture as I melt
in thy mystic soul;
Will know the supremest action, will feel the
divinest rest,
And I who was here an atom shall aggregate
the whole.

Then here is to Death, my darling! I drink of
the ripe, red wine;
And here is another beaker to coffin and
shroud and pall!
And here is unto the hour when my soul shall
fuse with thine
Through the circles of God's creation, and
be of the All-in-All!

CARYL

Come to my arms, O, Caryl! Come to my arms
    once more!
Let me thrill with the keen, quick rapture that
    ran through my veins of yore!
Let me know that I am forgiven for the duty I
    left undone
When thy bridal roses were blooming and thy
    bridal robe was spun.

The lilies of that lost summer are fragrant
    and fair once more;
The songs of that dim, dead summer are soft
    as they were of yore;
The sky of that sweet, slain summer bends
    over our star below
With all of the violet splendor and sparkle of
    long ago.

But, ah! for their mystic meaning and their se-
    cretest sense no more
Rhyme in with my reckless spirit as they did
    in the days of yore,
When the grace of thy glad, free presence, the
    light of thy loving eyes,
Touched all of the world with glory—the glory
    of Paradise!

I'd barter the keys of heaven—I'd trample
    them under feet,
For the thrillant touch of thy kisses, the throb
    of thy clasp, my sweet!
And, O, for thy true forgiveness and tender to
    hear thee tell,

I'd welcome the fire and fetters of the uttermost under-hell!
Then come to my arms, my Caryl, if it only a
  moment be!
Come to my arms, belovèd, and, O, let me
  melt in thee!

VIVIAN

Vivian!
Vivian!
Where are you now?
O, where are you now?
The soft golden hair has turned gray on my
  brow,
And my heart is no longer in trancefulest tune
With the roses and raptures of jubilant June.
This wonderful world holds a heaven and hell
'Twixt the christening-font and the funeral
  bell,
And my heaven was lost when you left me that
  morn
In the pride of your passion, the strength of
  your scorn.

Vivian!
Vivian!
Where are you now?
O, where are you now?
In the dust of desire you trampled your vow;
The ear of an adder you turned to my cries
For the kiss of her lips and the light of her
  eyes;
In the tingle of triumph you hurled me to hell

For the pleasure that lay in her passionate
    spell;
A harlot and homeless you left me that morn
'n the pride of your passion, the strength of
    vour scorn.

Vivian!
Vivian!
Where are you now?
O, where are you now?
I know that the cere-cloth is chill on your
    brow,
Afar where the floods of the Arkansas flow,
In the wild, mournful forests you slumber, I
    know—
In the wild, mournful forests and fens where
    you fled
When you knew that the heart of your darling
    was dead—
When she turned, in her weakness, a traitor to
    thee,
As you, in your weakness, turned traitor to
    me.

Vivian!
Vivian!
Where are you now?
O, where are you now?
Are you walking in glory upon the green brow
Of the heavenly highlands, beyond the blue
    bars
Of the sky that is blooming with beautiful
    stars?
Or, lashed with the scorpion-lashes of God,
Are you treading the plow-shares that Lucifer
    trod?
Or there, where the Arkansas rolls to the deep,
Is your spirit as well as your senses asleep?

Vivian!
Vivian!
Where are you now?
,   O, where are you now?
In my dreams I still feel your hot kiss on my
     brow—
In my dreams I still feel the old clasp of your
     palm,
And my spirit sweeps out into infinite calm;
And I know that my love is immortal, and I
Will rest on your heart when the world has
     swept by—
Will rest on your heart through the passionate
     years,
Beyond the pale phantom of Time and its
     tears!

PERCIVAL

Percival sprang to his saddle-tree
     When pansies were purple and grass was
          green,
And over the heathery hills went he
     To see his lily—his own Lurline.
He halted his horse by the sounding sea—
He halted his horse by the bounding sea,
And thought what a startling thing and strange
Was its constant, but ever inconstant, change:
     Roaring, raving, laughing. leaping,
     Shining, shouting, crying. creeping,
     Tinkling, throbbing, sighing, sleeping,
          .   Evermore—evermore!

He spurred his steed till he made it bleed,
  When pansies were purple and grass was
    green,
And rode over river and rock and mead
  To meet his lily—his own Lurline.
He watched the sky as he went his way,
Through grass and flowers and forests gay,
And thought what a startling thing and strange
Was its constant, but ever inconstant, change:
    Howling, scowling, glory-gleaming,
    Purpling, paling, splendor-streaming,
    Darkling, sparkling, beaming, dreaming,
          Evermore—evermore!

A year went 'round as he rode apace,
  And pansies were purple and grass was green,
Yet on he went in his glad young grace,
  To clasp his lily—his own Lurline.
He watched the sod as he watched the sky
While the seasons went with their banners by,
And thought what a startling thing and strange
Was its constant, but ever inconstant, change:
    Thrilling, chilling, snowflakes sifting
    On the dead leaves o'er it drifting,
    Glad and green and garland-lifting,
          Evermore—evermore!

He came to the castle one dreamy dawn,
  When pansies were purple and grass was
    green,
And after all he had undergone
  He kissed his lily—his own Lurline.
And he watched his bride with the eager eyes
Of one who wanders in Paradise,
And he thought what a sweet, sweet thing and
    strange
Was her constant, but never inconstant, change:
    Laughing, dancing, singing, blessing,

Helping, kissing and caressing,
True and tender love confessing,
          Evermore—evermore!

But came a wrathful and rainy morn,
  When pansies were purple and grass was
    green,
And he found his beautiful bride foresworn
  And a hell of fire their hearts between;
For change is written on sea and sod
And sky by the great, white hand of God,
But nothing is more inconstant than
The heart of woman or heart of man:
    Loving, thrilling, praying, yearning,
    Crying, pleading, calling, burning,
    Cursing, hissing, hating, spurning,
          Evermore—evermore!

PHILIP

Forgive thee, Philip? When the love slain by
    thy barbèd speech
  Shall rise from its red blood and live within
    my life once more,
Mayhap my heart will then relent—my hand
    to thine will reach—
          But not before.

Forgive? When my poor, perished hopes shall
    blossom in the dust
Where thou didst trample them that day,
    mayhap my weak soul will
Receive thy traitor-kisses with the old, mad,
    reckless trust—
          But not until.

A dead love is forever dead: no seraph can
    unseal
  Its sepulcher—nor God himself give back its
    vanished fire;
Its lost hopes are forever lost—no future can
    make real
          Their sweet desire.

I loved thee with a love that gave the second
    place to God,
  I held thy breast unto my breast, thy cheek
    unto my cheek,
I knelt and kissed the very dust whereon thy
    feet had trod,
          For I was weak;

Yet, knowing that through flood and flame for
    thee I'd gladly go,
  And knowing that with soul and sense I blind-
    ly worshiped thee—
Thou, with a traitor-hand, didst strike at me
    a deadly blow—
          Philip—at me!

Forgive thee, Philip! I will not forgive thee!
    It is sworn!
  Nor will I lure thee with a lie to please thy
    perjured heart;
I hate thee with a burning hate, and scorn
    with blasting scorn!
          Depart—depart!

IN AUGUST

O, that August dawn!
O, that August dawn!
How the sunfire sparkled on lake and lawn!
How the roses seemed drooping to kiss thy
    feet
As we went through the greenwood glad, my
    sweet!
How the lark went winging and warbling there,
Till lost at last in the argent air!
And, looking down in thine eyes divine,
I felt that forever thy thoughts were mine.

O, that August day!
O, that August day!
The sea in its splendor spread away
And away, till it vanished in vivid space
On shores of glory and shoals of grace;
While blended in one was thy spirit then
With mine in communion beyond our ken;
But looking down in thine eyes divine
I knew that forever thy heart was mine.

O, that August dusk!
O, that August dusk!
All subtle with scent of myrrh and musk,
And shaken with bulbul songs that beat
In silvery strains through their dim retreat,
And brave with the beauty of stars that shone
With a lusterful loveliness all their own;
And looking down in thine eyes divine
I felt that forever thy self was mine.

O, that August tide!
O, that August tide!
When I was blest, for thou wert my bride;
But it brought me bale as it brought me bliss,
For a poor, vain, fugitive life is this,
And ere that enchanted moon had fled
Thou wert lying dead—thou wert lying dead.

O, the August sun!
O, the August sun!
Its splendor into our sphere is spun,
And the August flowers are all aflame
With ravishing dyes that I cannot name,
And the August melody, balm and joy,
Once more the soul and the senses cloy,
But I am dead to their touch divine
As I kneel in tears at thy tranceful shrine.

O, the August hour!
O, the August hour!
Beyond the pale and beyond the power
Of mold and mortality, when I
Shall kiss and shall clasp thee by and by!
Is it a dream? Will it dawn for me—
That hour the living may never see,
When I can look in thine eyes divine
And know that forever thy soul is mine?

TO A DEAR, DEAD FRIEND

"No years to be,
No change from me,
    Thy memory can sever."

Valley-dimpled in the distance stretch the
stalwart mountain-lines,

Glorified by sunset-splendors, garlanded by
plumy pines;
Sheer below, within the purple and the pause
of twilight tide,
Spread the silent fields, far-reaching to the
forests wild and wide--
Spread the silent fields, where cattle browse
beside the saffron stream,
Where, in gold and green transplendent, the
triumphant harvests teem;
Where the flowers flash with beauties, borrowed
from the sky and sun
And by many a subtle process in their shining
petals spun;
Where the dim and dusty highway through the
hedges dippeth down
Past the pleasant old plantations, to the quaint
and quiet town.

Through and through my lattice tangled, burn
and shine the scarlet blooms,
Trembling with their bold, strange beauty,
tingling with their sweet perfumes;
Now and then the soft winds smite them, and
their spicy petals spill
On the open book that thrills me as no other
book can thrill—
Book wherein a grand old master, moldering
now within his grave,
Sets the whole, broad world and heaven to
a high, victorious stave.

But the miracle and marvel of the sunland
swimming there,
With its glory and its garlands, vanishes in
viewless air—
With its glory and its gladness, though the
twilight splendors still

Paint and plash the magic mountains where
the creamy cascades spill;
Still the soft winds smite the flowers, and their
fragrant petals fall
On the poems of the poet who has held me in
his thrall;
But the magic spell is broken, and the book
falls from my knee,
As across the cliffs and lowlands of our lovely
Tennessee,
Through the hush and through the half-light, fly
my faithful thoughts to thee.

Before I saw thee, Avery, I knew I'd like thee
well—
I like whoever speeds a spear for Reason
and for Right,
Who leads humanity to break the brutalizing
spell
Of prince and priest, and grandly march into
the white, glad light.

I knew thou wert in line and one with all who
dare defy
A crowned, and mailed, and sceptered wrong
—whate'er that wrong may be,
Who own no master here below, no master in
the sky,
And who would break all bars and gyves,
and bid the bond go free.

I knew I'd like, thee, Avery, before I saw thy
face,
But when at last I came within the magic of
thy spell,
And saw thy life in all its light—its grand and
simple grace—
I came to love thee with a love my tongue
can never tell.

I often could not hear thy words for looking
  in thine eyes—
They flashed a deeper depth of thought than
  any form of speech,
And often in our rougher moods I tempered
  my replies,
  Because thy tones had meaning that thy language did not reach;

Because I knew in all the world, in all the
  suns to be,
  Search where I might, or far or near, I nevermore would know
As true a friend, O, Avery! as tender a friend
  as thee,
  This side the dim, green place of rest, where
  white grave-roses blow!

For thou didst take me to thy heart—didst
  take me by the hand—
When friends of fairer days turned false, and
  hissed me down with hate,
And when I found my castles had been built
  upon the sand,
  And stormy waves had dashed and left their
  splendors desolate.

Mayhap, O, Avery! mayhap, the moons will
  wax and wane,
  And wax and wane a hundred times, within
  the secret skies,
And sear our hearts with passion-fires, and scar
  our hearts with pain
  Unspeakable, before we look within each
  other's eyes;

The frosts and flowers of long, long years our
  lives may lie between,

The lights on many a marriage-shrine may
    flash and fade away,
And the lily-bells may blossom, and the grasses
    quiver green
    Upon the tomb of many a friend before ,that
    distant day;

And seas all starry-isled may break between thy
    way and mine,
    Gray cliffs and green champaigns may lie be-
    tween our severed lands,
Above us alien skies may bend, and stranger
    stars may shine
    Upon our parted paths before we clasp each
    other's hands.

And mayhap, Avery, mayhap, we nevermore
    will meet
    In all the circling cycles that the awful ages
    hold,
For death may step between us, and it is a
    dream too sweet—
    That grand, all-hail Hereafter, far beyond
    the graveyard mold.

But yet whatever may befall—though moons
    and miles may part,
    Though buds may blow and grasses grow be-
    tween thy face and mine—
The love for thee shall leal be forever in my
    heart,
    And all its best impulses shall be thine—
    and only thine.

Thou hadst a subtle influence thou never yet
    hast known
    Upon my life, for when we met, so dark was
    my despair,

That all the aspirations from my stormy soul
    had flown,
And only stony Sorrow, with her ruined
    dreams, was there;

But to feel I had the friendship of a great,
    good heart like thine,
Was a promise and a prophecy of better
    things to be—
A radiant revelation that mayhap this life of
    mine
Would broaden into brighter ways, and
    worthier of thee;

And if I strike upon my harp a chord that yet
    shall ring
Responsive in the breasts of men; or if an
    occult flame
Shall touch my pen until its thoughts through
    all the world shall wing,
To thee, O, Avery! to thee, will I trace back
    my fame!

Thou wert my inspiration, and thou wilt for-
    ever be,
O, tenderest friend man ever had, and truest
    friend of mine,
And every canticle I sing, I consecrate to thee,
    With all the love of all a life that is forever
    thine.

THE LIGHT OF LIFE

(INSCRIBED TO GORDON L. SNEED.)

Through the magical lights loom the Cumber-
land mountains,
Clear-cut on the opaline sky-line away,
While down from their heights dash and thun-
der the fountains
That blossom and break into silvery spray!

Below, the glad gardens in sunlight are swimming
Through all the glad sweep of the summery
hours,
And wide-waving forests are blissfully brim-
ming
With lyrics of linnets and fire of flowers!

But, O! my heart turns to the beautiful places
Away, far away in the passionate past,
And, O! my heart yearns for the beautiful faces
That haunt my lost hours, and will to the
last.

    *   *   *   *   *

And when o'er purple sunset seas
The old day sadly drifts afar
I watch the first, faint, yellow star
Shine through the semi-tropic trees,

I think of those who loved me here,
And marvel will I clasp their hands
Once more within these lower lands,
Or in some vague, mysterious sphere.

I see the light of laughing eyes,
And hear the tender tones once more

That thrilled me in the years of yore,
Like a lost song from Paradise!

' When I look back upon those hours,
They hold me with a subtle spell—
Wherever their soft foot-prints fell
Bright blossom fair, supernal flowers.

We never know a happiness,
Until it layeth stark and sweet
Within its white, white winding-sheet,
Beyond the power our paths to bless.

O, friends, wherever ye may be
Within this weary world to-day—
In gilded cities far away
Or greenwoods mirrored by the sea—

Think not ye are forgotten yet,
For, till my pulses cease to beat,
Thy lives so gracious, pure and sweet,
My heart will nevermore forget;

And thou, for whom my harp is strung
Upon these mountain-heights to-day,
Know that the love will live for aye
That from our brief acquaintance sprung.

I love thy liberal mind—it takes
No swift misjudgments from the crowd;
But of itself, all pure and proud,
Its own and honest verdict makes.

Won was I by thy wit, but more,
Won by thy words of friendship warm
That took my very heart by storm
Within the summer that is o'er;

And if within the years to be
One act or utterance of mine

14

.   Can lighten any load of thine
I pray that thou wilt call to me;

For if I held it in my power
   O'er thee the bluest skies should bend
   Undarkened to the last, O, friend!
By any storms that ever lower.

The roses with their hearts of fire
   Should stoop and kiss thy very feet,
   And life with rapture be replete
In every fond dream and desire.

Out of the passions and the strife
   And hatreds crowding round my way,
   Confronting me from day to day,
I find the one sweet light of life

In knowing that I have a crown
   In fond and faithful hearts that dare
   Defend me from the spear and snare
Of devil-foes who hunt me down;

And knowing that I have a place
   In true and tender hearts like thine
   Has glorified this life of mine
With one sweet attribute of grace!

ULALIE

Severed, O, Lord! the silver cord that bound
   her unto life!
In white samite she sleeps to-night who should
   have been my wife.

O, Vasey Vane, beyond the main in tears and
    sackcloth bow—
The saintly maid thy wiles betrayed is pale
    and pulseless now.
From sneer and fleer to the starry sphere of
    Christ who was crucified
She passed away but yesterday, and now she
    is my bride.
Aye! ashes spread upon thy head for murdered
    Ulalie,
Yet, O, forgiven by man and heaven thou
    canst not hope to be—
For though forgiven by man, yet heaven will
    be avenged on thee!

I was a thrall of Sedgewood Hall, thou wert a
    prince of pride,
With stores of gold and slaves untold and fair
    possessions wide;
Yet I was blest, for she confessed her love at
    last for me;
Yet I was banned, for, O! her hand her father
    pledged to thee.
Wo worth that hour! Wo worth thy power,
    that ever it should be!
I seemed to trace upon her face a tender look
    of love,
Reflected now from her rapt brow, white lily-
    crowned above!
A look for me, and not for thee, false father
    of the dead!
A look for me, and not for thee, to whom she
    vainly plead:
Away! Away! Nor longer stay to weep her bier
    beside—
She is not thine, but only mine—forevermore
    my bride!

*   *   *   *   *

Kiss, sweetest, kiss me unto bliss—I twine
   within thy hair
These lily flowers from bridal bowers—they
   make thee look more fair!
Kiss, sweetest, kiss me unto bliss—I place upon thy hand
This bridal ring—now let us wing our way to
   distant land!
Kiss, sweetest, kiss me unto bliss!—O, God, I
   do but rave!
Within an hour my star and flower will lie
   within the grave!

*   *   *   *   *

O'er pines and peaks the shrill wind shrieks,
   while up the wrinkled sands
The haggard sea cries piteously and wrings
   and wrings its hands;
The moon looks out from her redoubt within
   the scowling sky,
What time the knell of passing-bell tolls
   from the chapel nigh.
The mass is said, they bear the dead with sol-
   emn tread away,
To sleep and sleep within its deep, dark home
   in churchyard clay,
Until the last long trumpet blast upon the
   Judgment-day,
And I am left of all bereft to walk my lonely
   way.

THE BUGLE

O, where, and O, where is the melody that
    rang
From out thy throat, O, bugle! in the battle
    clash and clang—
The fanfaron—the fanfaron that grandly swept
    and soared
While mangled men were shrieking and the
    thunder-guns uproared?

O, where, and O, where are thy strains that
    swept afar,
O'er dimpled cliffs and dewy coombs unto the
    morning-star,
As hounds and huntsmen followed where the
    Lord of Lisle led,
And gave thy golden throat a tongue before
    his arrow sped?
O, where, and O, where are thy many change-
    ful lays
That woke the magic echoes in those old me-
    morial days—
Thy victor-blasts in battle on the warfields of
    old France,
Thy joy-peals at the merry chase and revelry
    and dance?

Thy soft notes, thy sweet notes, when bridal-
    feast was spread,
Thy weird and wailing threnody that throbbed
    beside the dead,
Thy glad peal of thanksgiving that went ting-
    ling through the morn
When to the proud young Lord of Lisle a bon-
    ny heir was born?

O, where, and O, where hath thy music fled
    to-day?
O, hath it passed forever from the universe
    away?
Or through the circling cycles doth it wide
    and wider sweep,
And sing and surge forever on from purple
    deep to deep?

"It sings and it surges," the scientist replies,
"Beyond the blue horizon's rim, beyond the
    furthest skies,
Through all the countless centuries until the
    end shall be,
And not one note shall perish from its perfect
    harmony."

Then, O, and then, O, as its free strains float
    afar,
In mystic melody they break on many a bloom-
    ing star,
And the people, yes, the people in those
    strange, unspoken spheres,
May hear the music heard on earth within the
    ancient years.
O, bugle! O, bugle! upon the castle wall,
The men who lent thy lips their fire are
    stretched beneath the pall;
And never will thy golden throat possess a
    tongue again,
And never will thy torn lips thrill the blood of
    mortal men.

Yet, bugle, O, bugle! though we may not dis-
    cern
The strange truth and subtle truth, thy influ-
    ence eterne

Hath changed the very universe by starting on
    their way
Chime after chime of melody to surge and
    surge for aye.

Thus, bugle, O, bugle! my voice will never
    die,
And all the words I ever spake are sounding
    in the sky,
And they will sound forever on when I am ly-
    ing low
Within the tongueless silence of the sleep we
    all will know.

The lip-words, the lip-words and passion-
    words that tell
The loving or the loathing thoughts that deep
    within me dwell;
All these will sweep and circle on throughout
    infinity,
And thus am I immortal, though no after-life
    there be.

Immortal! Immortal! But what if I shall rise
From underneath the roses after Samæl seals
    mine eyes,
And stand before a judgment-bar what time
    my words proclaim
To all the hosts of all the worlds my glory or
    my shame?

ULRIC

This night, out-looking through my lattice-bars,
I see the pale procession of the stars,
   And hear the waters of the restless sea
Roll up the sands with slow, pulsating jars.

The landscape lies in a mysterious trance—
The gray peaks glimmer and the green leaves
      glance
   In the white moon-rays, while the vale below
A shadow vast and melancholy haunts.

Upon a ledge, beyond that gulf of gloom,
The village lights burst into silver bloom,
   As lornly down the wan rim of the west
Day vanishes with scarlet-streaming plume.

* *
*

I feel my spirit struggling with its chain,
I feel the links unrivet that restrain
   Its folded pinions—paradise this night,
This very night, the captive will regain.

And I am happy—for no wailing wife,
No clinging children hold me back to life,
   And make this time of death a time of dread,
Instead of joyful calm that follows strife.

I would not have a single faithful heart
To break; I would not have a tear to start;
   I would not have a moan be made for me—
Nay, none of these, as deathward I depart.

I would not leave a heritage of woe,
To those I love—to those who love me so—

The thought would mock, the thought would
    madden me
Upon the heights of heaven—this I know.

Far better as it is; I pass away
Into the golden light beyond the gray,
    Without one tie that knits me to my kind,
Without one hope or fear to bid me stay;

With no wan figures flying to and fro,
Wringing their hands and mourning as they
    go,
Crying to Christ, with wet, uplifted eyes,
And agonizings to avert the blow.

Instead, I hear the south wind softly stray
In through my casement from the fields away—
    The fragrant fields of asphodel—I hear
The bulbul singing low its sweetest lay;

While tender memories come back to me
Of a far time that nevermore will be,
    Of sounding forests by a shining flood,
And fond young friends who walked the world
    with me.

* *
*

The moments of my life are nearly told.
I sink—I swoon—I waken to behold
    The faces of my lost, belovèd ones,
Long hidden by the violets and mold.

Beyond the planets and the purple space
They beckon to me from a palm-green place,
    Where seas of splendor roll, where upward
    rise
The citadels of Christ in golden grace.

And while I watch, the harp of Israel
Sounds through the   universe!—The charmèd
    spell
Of time is broken!—Friends, I come! I come!

* *
*

And with the brave knight Ulric it was well.

CHICAGO

Once in the dreams, the vast, vague dreams,
    of a singer strong, there came
A vivid vision of unknown lands, over un-
    known leagues away;
And Prophecy fired his inner-soul with her own
    immortal flame,
    And made forecast of the miracles we realize
    to-day.

He saw him the lands, new, marvelous, in the
    Wonder West; and, lo!
They spread from the passionate zone of sun
    to the pulseless zone of snow

And midway there were the plains where we
    Walk in our pride to-day; ;
And the valleys of verdure fair and free,
    That swept to the sky away,
        To the jasper rim,
        Far, vast and dim,
    Of the splendorful sky away.

He saw it just as it came from God
    In the glad, fresh-morning years,

With never a grave in its soft, green sod,
  And never a trace of tears;

And never a crime, with its trail of red
  Heart's blood on the blossoms there,
And never a hiss of hate that sped
  To poison the sweet, pure air.

But a soul was missing from cliff and scar,
  From the woodland and the wave;
And the solitude—it was sadder far,
  Than is any grief or grave;

For the voice of man was unknown—unknown
  As it trembled in tones of love
And linked the land with the Glory-Throne
  Of God, in the Blue above.

Unknown were the sacrifices high,
  Unselfish and true and sweet,
That leadeth a man for his love to die
  In the dust at his loved one's feet.

Unknown were all the impulses proud,
  Immaculate and sublime;
The Honor that would prefer a shroud
  To a scepter that's bought with crime.

Unknown the surrender that self hath made,
  The loyalty to a trust,
That walks through the fierce flames unafraid
  For a cause that it knows is just.

And hark! As the singer looks, his hand
  On his harp is laid, and he
Smiting its strings, upsings a grand,
  Great song of a time to be:

Hosanna! Lift up the bright palm branches
  higher,

For man marches forward through flood and
    through fire,
Till there, on those beautiful prairies untrod,
He shall feel on his forehead the glory of God.

His hand shall transfigure that wilderness till
A CITY OF SPLENDOR, with progress athrill,
Like magic shall rise, and its radiant birth
Be a tale that is uttered all over the earth.

Its light shall sweep onward and out through
    the world,
Till the last chain is broken and battle-flag
    furled,
And Liberty rules in all realms, and the race
Leaves the gutters and gloom for the glory and
    grace,
And the serfs, as their equals, their sovereigns
    face.

    He hath passed to fields Elysian,
      He, the singer and the seer,
    But the City of his Vision—
      IT IS HERE!

AGNOSTIC ARGUMENTS

All things are unreal, or probably all things are unreal; and that is agnosticism.—HUXLEY.

AGNOSTICISM

Agnostic:
Let others bow at marble shrine
Within the white cathedral's calm,
And sing the penitential psalm,
And quaff the red communion-wine;
But never to your unseen King
Will my proud spirit bend the knee

Until with mortal eyes I see
An angel hovering on the wing,

Or hear a melody divine
Down-ringing through the purple skies,
Or see the fronded palms that rise
Where heaven's hills are said to shine.

Priest:
Vain child! Vain, boastful child! The day
That comes to all will come to thee,
And thou wilt quickly summon me
For thy blind, struggling soul to pray.

Agnostic:
Your God has said his law shall be
Fixed and inflexible—shall last
Until the endless end is past,
And yet you boldly hint to me

That when my light of life shall burn
· Low in the socket, by a strange
And priestly power you may change
Fulfillment of his laws eterne.

Priest:
Nay, nay! Not I. But if a soul
Repents of folly, sin and crime,
Though hovering on the verge of time,
God may relent and make it whole.

Agnostic:
He may? So his decrees divine
Are what he says they are not? He
May alter them for you or me
At a weak word of yours or mine?

Priest:
Thy quibble, sir, is crude and trite—

Agnostic: —
  But never has been answered yet;
  Pray clear it up, and you shall get
  A guinea for your church to-night.

Priest:
  It was not meant that he should make
  His seeming inconsistency
  Consistent unto thee or me—

Agnostic: —
  A most convenient cut to take!

Priest:
  Rash one! O, rash, misguided one!
  Thy scoffing stings me for thy sake,
  Thou must thy peace with heaven make,
  Or be forevermore undone!

Agnostic:
  O, Justice! Mercy! Love and Truth!
  You'say I must believe or be
  Tormented through eternity!
  A very pretty plan, forsooth.

  A very pretty plan, for I
  Without the gift of faith was born;
  And hold in great, consummate scorn
  A thing that I believe a lie!

  My reason rises to proclaim
  Against your Bible. Shall I be
  Held guilty? Speak! Who gave to me
  The reason that rejects the same?

Priest:
  Blind youth! Thy God gave unto thee
  Thy reason; but he likewise gave
  His revelations, strong to save—

Agnostic:—
   And still your two and two make three.
   I read the revelations. Then
      I read the rocks, the stars, the laws
      Pertaining to result and cause,
   And found myself at sea again.

   The stars cried out to me that they
      Had been belied by Bible-lore;
      The rocks told that the world was hoar
   With age in your Adamic days;

   Result said had there been a cause
      To drown our world, the water still
      Would kiss the very highest hill
   By all the plain, eternal laws.

   I read the revelations. There
      Troop men, who, if they lived to-day
      Would in our convict quarters lay
   Or from a scaffold swing in air.

   Their hands with human blood were wet,
      They held their slaves in galling gyves,
      Each had a harem full of wives,
   Each had a host of harlots, yet

   Your great God blessed their words and
      ways
      And sounded their exceeding worth
      In thunder-tones through all the earth,
   And lengthy drew he out their days.

   I read the revelations. There
      I found that God foreknows the fate
      Of every soul—its last estate,
   Its rapture or its mad despair;

   Yet, knowing this, he breathes the fire
      Of life into our nostrils; he

Makes millions far too weak to flee
The first demands of fierce desire;

They yield, and as I sweep these flies
From off my table does he sweep
Into eternal hell, where leap
Eternal flames, the great and wise

And beautiful and strong and brave—
And with this shining throng are hurled
The lees and rinsings of the world—
"A remnant only" will he save!

Priest:
O, son! O, mad, rebellious son!
One fact thy sophistries will rend,
We are free agents —

Agnostic: —
Christian friend,
Thy logic is too loosely spun.

Your church shall have my house and land
If you will harmonize for me
Free-knowledge with free-agency,
And I will join your Christian band.

How can a man be free to take
The right hand or the left, if God
Foresaw the path that would be trod?
Will he reverse it for our sake,

And thereby demonstrate that he
Did not foresee it, and thereby
Prove his omniscience a lie?
My Christian friend, it cannot be.

Priest:
Proud worm! thy blasphemy hath chilled
My very blood; but I will pray

For thy lost soul from day to day
That with the truth it may be thrilled.

Agnostic:
Yet, O! what would that heaven be
If when I stood within its calms,
Beneath its bright, immortal palms
The awful knowledge came to me

That I would never any more
Meet with a lost, beloved one,
Who was my life, my joy, my sun,
My all upon this lower shore;

That even to the endless end
He writhed within your hell, while I
Upon the hills of heaven high
To him no comfort sweet could send?

Priest:
Blind youth, the shrieks of those who fall
Will sound as music in your ears
And happier make the holy spheres,
When we shall understand it all.

Agnostic:
It will? O, black, accursed thought!
Let blank annihilation be
My fate before my soul shall see
This miracle upon it wrought!

Rejoice to hear the cries of one
I held in rapture to my heart,
Who was of me a very part
Before my mortal race was run?

Far rather would I rush into
The very fangs of hell, and there
His agonies unending share
Than prove to friendship so untrue.

Priest:
 Rejecting God and all that lies
 Beyond the grave-stone—

Agnostic: —
 Hold, good sir!
 Although I am no worshiper
 Of things unseen within the skies,

I nathless hold that there may be
 A Lord and Master of the spheres,
 Who guides the glory of the years
And supervises you and me,

I hold that we may live when earth
 From under us shall swing; but, lo,
 There is no jot of proof to show
That we shall have a second birth.

There never has a whisper sped
 From out the moonless mists that weep
 Forever o'er the clanging deep
That crawleth outward with our dead;

And as we grander knowledge gain
 The more distinctly we descry
 That nature gives your God the lie
(Or *vice versa*) pat and plain.

And thus I cast no horoscope
 Of what the future holds in store
 When all this hurly-burly's o'er;
And, if my bosom holds a hope,

It buds and blossoms from a strange
 And mystic feeling in my heart
 That mortal life is but a part
Of a transcendent whole, whose range

Shall reach through endless æons where
　　Each soul, though cankered o'er with
　　　crime,
May scale the highest heights sublime
From out the depths of blank despair.

A dream, mayhap, for every man
　　Is more or less a fool, you know,
　　Is swayed by folly to and fro,
And has been since the world began.

WHY?

　　O, where is my little Lily?—
　　My lost love, where is she?
Will never a god or never a man in the uni-
　　verse answer me?
In the blossom years of my sweet, slain youth,
　　on a morning hour like this,
I pressed on her red, upreaching lips a pas-
　　sionate farewell kiss;
Then I watched her ship go sailing afar out
　　over the golden rim,
While a lark soared up from its low, green
　　nest with a glad thanksgiving hymn;
And the scent of the oleander-flowers was sweet
　　on the summer air,
And a serpent slid through the tangled grass
　　and hissed at the glory there!

　　O, where is my little Lily?—
　　My lost love, where is she?
Is she dead in the Sunland far away that she
　　answereth not to me?

Does she sing on the high hill-crests of Christ,
   and lost in the rapture there,
Has she forgotten the vows she spake on the
   beautiful cliffs of Clare,
When a secret influence seemed to blend her
   soul and my soul in one,
While we melted away in the ardent bliss of
   blossom and song and sun?
Does she clang the fetters of hell to-day, and,
   lost in a last despair,
H s she forgotten our bridal-kiss on the beautiful cliffs of Clare?
Or does she sleep an unending sleep where the
   jasmine-flowers wave,
And draw their color and flash and scent from
   her dead heart in the grave?

Speak not, speak not of the bleeding God upon that cruelest tree!
Speak not of His infinite love for man, of His
   infinite love for me!
He has torn the heart from my bosom, He has
   trampled it under-feet,
He has taken out of my life the life and the
   love that made it sweet;
Then why should I thrill with a rapt delight
   when the tale of His love is told?
Or why should I weep that the Roman spears
   were red with His blood of old?
Why did He fashion me as He did—a being of
   flesh and fire,
And dower me with the flower of love, and the
   flame of a sweet desire—
And dower me with the flower of love to lay
   on a dead girl's breast,
And the flame of a sweet desire to burn o'er
   the shrine where she lies at rest?

IF I WERE GOD!

Immortal should all of mortality be
    If I were God;
Infinite all that is finite in thee,
    If I were God;
The luminous lilies forever should shine,
The golden grapes drip with a delicate wine,
The red roses flame on the lush, trailing vine,
    If I were God.

The song-birds should lilt in an evergreen
    bower,
    If I were God;
And twitter and trill thro' an eveningless hour,
    If I were God;
And never a leaf in the green forest gay
Be borne from its bough, for no dark, wintry
    day,
Nor black, thunder-tempests rise wild in our
    way,
    If I were God.

Never a heart should be broken on earth,
    If I were God;
Never a misery follow our mirth,
    If I were God;
Never should longings be vile or vain,
Never be pestilence, famine or chain,
Never be poverty, farewells or pain,
    If I were God.

The fires of friendship should faithfully burn,
    If I were God;
Heart unto heart should unchangingly turn,
    If I were God;

The senses should reel with the sweetest de-
   light,
The rapturous passions of sin should be right,
And law with the sunburst of liberty bright,
      If I were God.

The dreams be fulfilled of the poets and sages,
      If I were God.
And all the grand yearnings of infinite ages,
      If I were God;
The march of Humanity, strong and sublime,
Should ring with the footfalls of angels in
   rhyme,
And Reason be regnant in every clime,
      If I were God.

RUTH

"Kenneth, hand my harp to me,
   I will set its spirit free."

Then she swept its strings, and I
Saw a sweet song flash and fly—
   Flash from out the bannered room,
   Fly into the golden gloom,
Far into the soundless sky,
   Till it came unto a star
   Where the lost who love us are;
And I saw the glad, white gleam
   Of the asphodels, and there
   Was an angel bright and bare.
Beautiful! The Christ may dream,
   But he cannot realize
The fine splendor of the face,

Nor the glory of the eyes,
Nor the strange, magnetic grace
  Of the angel standing there
  Beautiful and bright and bare!

Suddenly I saw him start
  With a swift and sad surprise
  Glowing in his guilty eyes,
As the song fell on his heart,
  As it kissed his lips and sang—
  As it clasped his limbs and sang:

The miracle-mornings come back to me
  As they came in the marvelous moons of old,
With the same glad flash of the laughing sea,
  And the same green ferns in the laughing
      mold,
With the same strange birds from the sunlands
      far,
  And the same blithe songs that we knew so
      well,
With the same pure rays of our mystic star
  In the dewy heart of the lily-bell!
Yes! All that I loved come back to me
  But I see them not through thy loving eyes:
If their God were gone could the angels see
  The old same beauty in Paradise?

O, Percy, my prince! if I only knew
  No seraph had stolen thy heart from me!
But, ah! if the living are oft untrue,
  Who knows that the dead will truer be?
Who knows? For, O! in that mystic star
  The women are fairer by far than I,
And love with a passion intenser far
  Than the heart that died when it felt thee die.
And, mayhap, I never will know the bliss
  That we knew in the blossomy Junes of old—

Thy darling clasp and thy dirling kiss,
And the whisperless joy of a joy untold!
A cloud crawled over the charmèd-star
Where the beautiful lost who love us are;
A cry rang down through the golden gloom,
A silence fell in the bannered room,
The fountain plashed as it plashed before.
The nightingale sang in the myrtle tree,
A soul flashed out of the open door,
And the world was a dead, waste world to me!
I reeled to the side of the singer there—
Dead—dead in the splendor and flush of
youth!
"O, Ruth!" I cried to her," O, my Ruth!"
And I fell at her feet and I kissed her hair,
And I laid my lips on her bosom bare;
For, ah! I had loved her in vain while she
Had loved a lover in Paradise:
He was false to her—she was false to me—
And a god sits up in the golden skies!

IF I THOUGHT AS YOU THINK

Why do you cling unto life, my brothers?—
why do you cling unto life? I say—
Why do you weep when the yoke and fetters
of flesh from a dear friend drop away?
You know this world is a House of Sorrow,
you know this world is a House of Sin,
That pain is the Dead Sea fruit of pleasure,
and will be ever as it hath been.
Why, then, cling unto life, when over the blue,
transpicuous rim afar

Shineth the walls of the Wondrous City where
    only blessings and blisses are?
Why do you beat your hands with passion,
    and storm the sky with your plea and
    prayer,
Whenever passes a stainless spirit forever out
    of your clasp and care?
You say he goes to a glad, brave kingdom over
    a vague and voiceless sea,
Where never a last good-bye is spoken and
    never and never a grave shall be,
And where from rapture to perfect rapture with
    crown and lyre he soars and sings,
The chrism of Christ upon his forehead, the
    glory of God upon his wings.
If I thought as you think, my brothers, if I
    believed in a better sphere
Beyond the grass and the golden lilies that
    blossom over a dead man here,
I would tingle with great, strange gladness
    whenever a friend of mine should die,
I would robe him in festal raiment and I would
    kiss him a gay good-bye;
And, O! when unto me comes the hour—the
    miracle-hour that comes to all—
Never a cypress branch or blossom should throw
    its gloom on my gorgeous pall;
At my funeral should be dancing, and dainty
    feasting at festal board;
Should be singing and jest and laughter and
    gurgle of wine in the glasses poured,
And jubilant bells should rock the steeples
    when I was borne to the gay, bright
    grave,
And rattle of drums and trill of trumpets blend
    in a glad thanksgiving stave!

THE LAND OF FANCY-FREE

Beyond the Hills Delectable—wherever they
    may be—
And far beyond the moon-down, the sun-
    down and the mist,
In sempiternal beauty lies the Land of Fancy-
    Free,
    And thither go my gladdest Thoughts to hold
      their happy tryst.
But how they go and when they go I'm sure I
    cannot say,
    For quicker than the flicker of a star-flash
      they are there,
Where fields of golden lilies spread to creamy
    cliffs away,
    And foam of yellow sunbeams bubble in the
      roses rare;
And there they dance and revel over flower-
    bells and ferns,
    And bump against the butterflies that flitter
      to and fro,
And drink from honeysuckle cup the dew that
    in it burns,
    And help the blithe, capricious wind her
      bugle-horn to blow.
They whistle with the mocking-bird a merry,
    madsome lay,
    And ride upon the thistle-down a waltzing up
      the air,
And slide upon the gossamers that dangle from
    the spray,
    And tumble with the bumble-bees o'er bridal
      blossoms fair.

O. Land of Fancy-Free, O, Land of Fancy-
Free!
O, sunny, funny, jolly, folly Land of
Fancy-Free!
O, whether I'm a-waking or asleep, away
from me
My thoughts oft go a-trooping with their
golden harps to thee!

    *   *   *   *   *

Hark! Suddenly they hear a lyre upringing to
the sky,
Another and another chime in the chorus
strong,
And, lo! the laureled singers of the centuries
sweep by,
And all the Land of Fancy-Free is quivering
with song!

And now my Thoughts with rapture unspeaka-
ble uprise,
And gaze upon the godlike brow of Homer
as he sings.
And search the searchless deeps divine of
Shakespeare's shining eyes,
And hear the tranceful tones of Poe—the Poet-
king of kings!
O, Land of Fancy-Free! O, Land of Fancy-
Free!
O, glorious, victorious, glad Land of
Fancy-Free!
O, all the grand and gifted who have been
and who will be,
Will sing and soar forever in the Land of
Fancy-Free!

    *   *   *   *   *

The poets pass; through soul and sense there
leap electric thrills

Of rapt delight: my Thoughts forget the
  tears that I have wept,
As softly o'er the sapphire rim and down the
  shining hills
Troop all my glorious, sweet friends who in
  the grave have slept;
And O, the highest height of heaven is less
  transplendent far
Unto my Thoughts than is the fair, fresh
  Land of Fancy-Free.
As through the sylvan valleys, over purple cliff
  and scar
They walk in company with those who were
  the world to me.
The wreaths of locust-blossoms bend above
  them as they pass.
And down the rays of sunlight trickle bird-
  songs from the air,
And daisies white and dew-drops bright are
  laughing in the grass.
And all the ecstasies of earth are blent with
  heaven there!
  O, Land of Fancy-Free! O, Land of Fancy-
    Free!
  O, kissful, blissful, olden, golden Land of
    Fancy-Free!
  If in the timeless Time afar an After-life
    there be,
  O, may my soul its pinions plume and
    soar away to thee!
      *   *   *   *   *
If I must live forever, let me live where sense
  hath part
With the spirit in the blessings that shall
  blossom for my heart:
If I must live forever, let me live where I will
  know

My friends—and know them as they were within these lands below—
With all the fire and sweet desire that thrilled
  them here below, .
Without one change that will estrange the
  earthly ties of old,
Before the funeral-hymn was sung, the funeral-
  bell was tolled.
If I must live forever, let me live where I will
  find
The gifted men and women whom no priestly
  gyves could bind,
For though their garments trailed in sin, their
  genius broke the spell
That held the masses captive in the mediæval
  hell,
And gave to voiceless thoughts a tongue, to
  nerveless swords a flame,
And led the legions on and up from servitude
  and shame.
    If I must live forever, O! let that forever
      be
    A jocund, joyful, jolly life in Land of
      Fancy-Free!
    No walled and gated, golden-plated Para-
      dise for me,
    Where all the pious feather-pates and
      Puritans will be;

No, none of that for me!—no, none of that for
  me!
But the blessings and caressings of the Land
  of Fancy-Free;
Where we will hold communion high upon
  a common plane
With old Voltaire and Ingersoll, with Shelley
  and Tom Paine;

Hear Byron's matchless timbrel ring against
    all sham and shames,
And see the Heretics who died in the devour-
    ing flames;
Keep step in time with Washington and grand,
    old Robert Lee,
And all the Rebels of the world in land of
    Fancy-Free!
O, Land of Fancy-Free! O, Land of Fancy-
    Free!
Where never is a prison-house, nor chain,
    nor scaffold-tree!
Where thought and deed and sweet desire
    forever shall be free,
And every dream of soul and sense reality
    shall be!

QUESTIONINGS

I wonder when the spirit
    Leaves the flesh and bone that bound it
      To the passions of our planet
      And the raptures of our race,
If it sees its poor, lost body,
    With the loving arms around it;
      If it quivers with the kisses
      On the pure and pallid face'

I wonder if it listens
    To the praises of the pastor;
      Hears him say the dead has risen
      To the Sunland of the Soul,
While it knows the secret sinnings

Of the thing that was its master
  Rise with flaming swords to drive it
  From the glory and the goal!

I wonder if it watches
  Till it sees the dead forgotten—
    Sees new friends usurp the favor
    Of the hearts that were its own;
If it looks below the daisies
  Where the grave-worm is begotten—
    Where the eyeless skull is grinning
    At a jest to us unknown!

I wonder if the truth is
  That the spirit can remember
    All its pains and all its passions,
    All its terrors and its tears,
Stealing swiftly on its vivid
  Summer visions, as November
    Crashes down in storm and darkness
    On the splendor of the years!

No! ah, no! Far better for us
  That we die, and die forever—
    That we slip into the shadows
    And the silences eterne,
Than be hunted down and haunted,
  When the soul and sense dissever,
    With the memories that mock us
    In this lower life inferne!

I bring you, Basil, a dewy rose
From under the Mississippi skies,
As sweet as the strange, sweet breath that
blows
O'er the glory-gardens of Paradise;

"As red as the red, bright blood that crept
To the face of Margery, flower-fair,
When close to your hot, young heart she
slept—
Her bright hair tangled within your hair.

"It bloomed from her bosom, and its hue
Was sucked from her dead heart in the
dust—
A heart whose every throb was true,
Till you, O, Basil! betrayed its trust!"

*   *   *   .   *   *

Heigh-ho! old fellow, the dead is dead—
The past is past. There is no return,
And what is a rose from a wormy bed,
Though its leaves with the blood of a lover
burn?

A trifle—for human clay is clay,
And men and women are nothing more
Than creatures that crawl through a little day,
And die when that little day is o'er.

The beautiful bird, upsoaring there,
Knows every passion a king can know—
He has mourned his mate with a dumb de-
spair,
And yet we pity him not—O, no!

He tingles with love and lust, has known
    The hissing hate of a human heart,
Would bravely die to defend his own—
    In all things proving our counterpart;

And yet the ball from your rifle sings,
    And the poor thing drops to the daisied sod—
A quiver sharp of its soft, white wings,
    And its innocent life goes back to God.

Well! it was made for your bullet, just
    As my dead girl under the old rose-tree
Was made for me from the fire and dust
    To die from the fire and dust of me!

I hold that whatever is, is wrong;
    If there was no God in his glory-sphere,
The sin that is sinewy and strong
    Would never revel and riot here.

If there was no life there would be no lust,
    No daggers red with the blood of men;
No treason unto a tender trust,
    Nor chain, nor scaffold, nor prison pen;

Nor arrow speeding through amber skies,
    To cleave a caroling heart in twain,
No tiger-beasts with their burning eyes,
    To suck the blood from a pulsing vein.

But I was brought to this ball of mud,
    That swings in the interstellar skies,
The flame of passion within my blood,
    And sweet temptations before mine eyes.

My very strength was a spur to sin,
    And the God up there in the golden sky
Had set the toils- -if I tumbled in
    Who was to blame for it—he or I?

But life will leave us, and we become
A handful of dust in this flying star,
Buried forever in darkness dumb,
    Just as the serpents that sting us are

What will I know of my treason then?
    What does she know of my treason now?
What does she know of that old day when
    I lightly laughed at my ring and vow?

Nothing, old fellow, and when I die,
    And the grass of an hundred years is green,
Nobody living will know that I
    Have been to-day or have ever been;

And nobody dead will ever know
    That Margery fell through her trust in me—
And the suns will go and the suns will glow,
    Though the dead girl blooms in the old rose-
        tree.

Heigh-ho! old fellow, your scruples bring
    A smile to this sunny heart of mine;
Fling down the rose!—'Tis a trifling thing—
    And fill you a beaker brave with wine.

We will drink to the things divine that be,
    To the diamond mornings we still enjoy,
To the flowery sod and the foaming sea,
    And the lovely women who live, my boy!

THE NEW SERMON

O! long hath the white bridal-altar
    To thee been a glittering goal,

Though hobble its pledges and halter
    And harry and hamper the soul;
O, higher thy aim, and O! higher
    Thy object in living should be,
For dust is the wage of desire,
    And death its decree!

Then spurn it, and turn from its pathway
    Of quicksands, though brilliant with
       blooms,
At the last ye will find it a wrath-way
    Of curses, or hearses and tombs.
Though the crimes that be crimson and
    carnal
The babes on thy bosom forego,
They will lie at the last in a charnel,
    All lampless and low.

This life is a tragedy ever,
    But over its awfulest years
There shineth a glory that never
    Goes out in a tempest of tears;
There be that will nevermore perish
    The beautiful, good and the true,
And these be the things ye should cherish,
    While sense ye subdue.

O! rare will our lasting reward be,
    And reach o'er the rim of the tomb,
And never by shame, nor by sword, be
    Despoiled, nor cut down in its bloom;
While ye who are led by the lying,
    Sweet lures of the sense, will be left
Over many a coffin-lid crying,
    "Bereaved and bereft!"

PER CASTRA AD ASTRA

"Per castra ad astra"—through camps to the
  stars—
Ran the demagogue legend of old:
It glowed on the banners borne forth to the
  wars
By the soldiers believing and bold.

When torn by the spears of the truculent foe,
And trampled by hoof and by heel,
They were taught that their glorified spirits
  would go
Straightway to the Land of the Leal.

Poor dupes of proud devils! They thought if
  they gave
Of their blood to the glory of kings
They would sweep forth, transfigured, from out
  of the grave
With a flash of white, fluttering wings!

Per castra ad astra"—the lie has come down
Through cycles and conquests unknown;
And still it stirs men to march forth for the
  crown,
And with bayonets prop up the throne;

And still it stirs many to barter the bloom
And the song and the sunlight of time,
For the hope of a blessing beyond the bleak
  tomb
In a vague and invisible clime:

To stifle the lyric that leaps from the heart,
And to turn from the waltzers away,

Though thrilling and tingling to share in a
    part
Of the merriment gladsome and gay;

To shrink from a present and palpable bliss
    And many a blessing benign;
To flee from the sweet, cunning lips that would
    · kiss,
And the ripe, rosy sparkle of wine.

Yes, they hiss down the flesh and its every
    delight,
    And they dream the denial will buy
A lily-hung harp and a diadem bright
    In a possible sphere in the sky.

O! pity the Puritan friar and nun,
    Who crucify sense for the soul;
Who tread upon thistles while under the sun,
    And quaff of the bitterest bowl.

O! pity the martyrs, wherever they are,
    Who sacrifice happiness here;
Who boast of the pleasures they mangle and
    mar
    In their wrath on the altars they rear;

For the grave-worms are cruel, the grave-clods
    are chill,
    And a dream is uncertain at best;
Then laugh and make merry, my lads, with a
    will,
    While the passions pulse high in the breast;

Nor trade off the glorious things that you hold
    In the grip of your palms for a prize
That may vanish forever away when the mold
    Sets its seal on your beautiful eyes.

Be good to yourselves, and be good unto all
Who travel your way to the tomb,
And reach out wherever your foot-prints may
    fall
For all of the roses that bloom.

Seek the glad, whitest glory of starlight and
    sun,
And when it is lost in the night
Let your hearts bubble over with frolic and fun
Where the festival fires burn bright.

Kiss the lips that may offer, and kiss them
    once more,
And join in the shout and the song,
And drink of the dew that the wine-presses
    pour,
And jest as you journey along.

"Per castra ad astra" may do for the clown,
But never for you or for me,
Till a dead man or woman from heaven wings
    down
And points up a path we can see!

UNFULFILLED

Once in my far, fresh morning years I dreamed
    of a day to be,
When out of the infinite inner soul a passion
    would come to me,
As the dayspring comes to the dreary world, as
    the blossom to the tree.

When the one sweet soul of all other souls
    would certainly find my own.
When the one true heart of all other hearts
    would certainly find my own,
And never again in all the world would I wan-
    der its ways alone.

O! I was a boy in that bright, old time, that
    seems like a dream to-day;
That seems like the dream of an alien life, in
    an alien land away;
A land in a star, in an orbit far, where gods
    in their glory stay.

Yes, I was a boy, and I thought our life was
    a beautiful life—ah, me!
The gilding drops from our gods divine, and
    the terrible truth we see,
That our world is a world of rot and dust—no
    matter how fair it be!

A touch of time in my raven hair, yet never
    the one rare thrill
Went out from my heart to another heart, and
    I know that it never will,
For age is coming apace, alack! and, oh! it is
    . calmly chill.

Under a green magnolia tent, in the golden
    moon-rays, I
Saw the ghost of myself, one nameless night,
    in a summer that has swept by;
Saw the ghost of my old, old self, and I sank
    to the sod with a low, quick cry;

For I stood before me just as I was in the
    sparkle and bloom of life,
Before I had broken my battle sword in its
    cruel, uncanny strife,

Flushed with a rosy, immortal hope—instinct
    with a radiant life!

The vision vanished, but oh! the dull, mad
    pain that it left with me,
As I thought of the thoughtless and thrillant
    boy—the boy who had once been me!
He was dead with all of his hopes divine—the
    boy who had once been me!

'Twixt my life that is, and my life that was,
    are the roses and frost of time,
The gods dethroned that I worshiped once,
    and festered with serpent slime,
The shrines despoiled where I brought my
    flowers in that old, old folly time.

'Twixt my life that is, and my life that was,
    is many a green, low grave
That marks the place where I bade good-bye
    to the beautiful and the brave:
Ah! the whole wide universe centers at last
    in the grave—in the cruel grave!

On through the empty and awful years I go
    where we all must go;
Back of me blossom the fairest fields that my
    feet will ever know—
Still here and yonder a star shines out, or a
    cluster of lilies blow.

Still here and there is a hand outreached, and
    a kind voice calls to me,
And a gleam of the olden glory falls like a flash
    on the sod and sea,
And my heart goes out with a glad, sweet throb
    to thee and to friends like thee!

WHAT WILL IT MATTER?

O! Fate is cruel, and Fate is cold,
  And only giveth a grave at last;
And what is glory, or love, or gold,
  When this brief hour is overpast?

What doth it matter us how we live?
  What doth it matter us how we die!
What can all of the future give
  When under the grassy clods we lie?

What will it matter to you and me—
  Insensate there in immortal calm—
Whether our funeral dirge shall be
  A reptile's hiss or a nation's psalm?

Nhat will it matter us then, I say,
  Whether a kingly crown we wore,
Whether we toiled from day to day,
  Or begged a pittance from door to door?

What will it matter us then if we
  Kept our garments from things impure,
Scattered our gold with a glad hand free,
  And walked in the strength of our worth
    secure;

Or whether we wallowed in lies and lust,
  And washed our palms in the blood of
    men,
And proved a traitor to every trust—
  What will it matter unto us then?

Whether our friends were false or true,
  Whether our foes were strong or weak,
What will it matter to me or you,
  After our candle is out? O, speak!

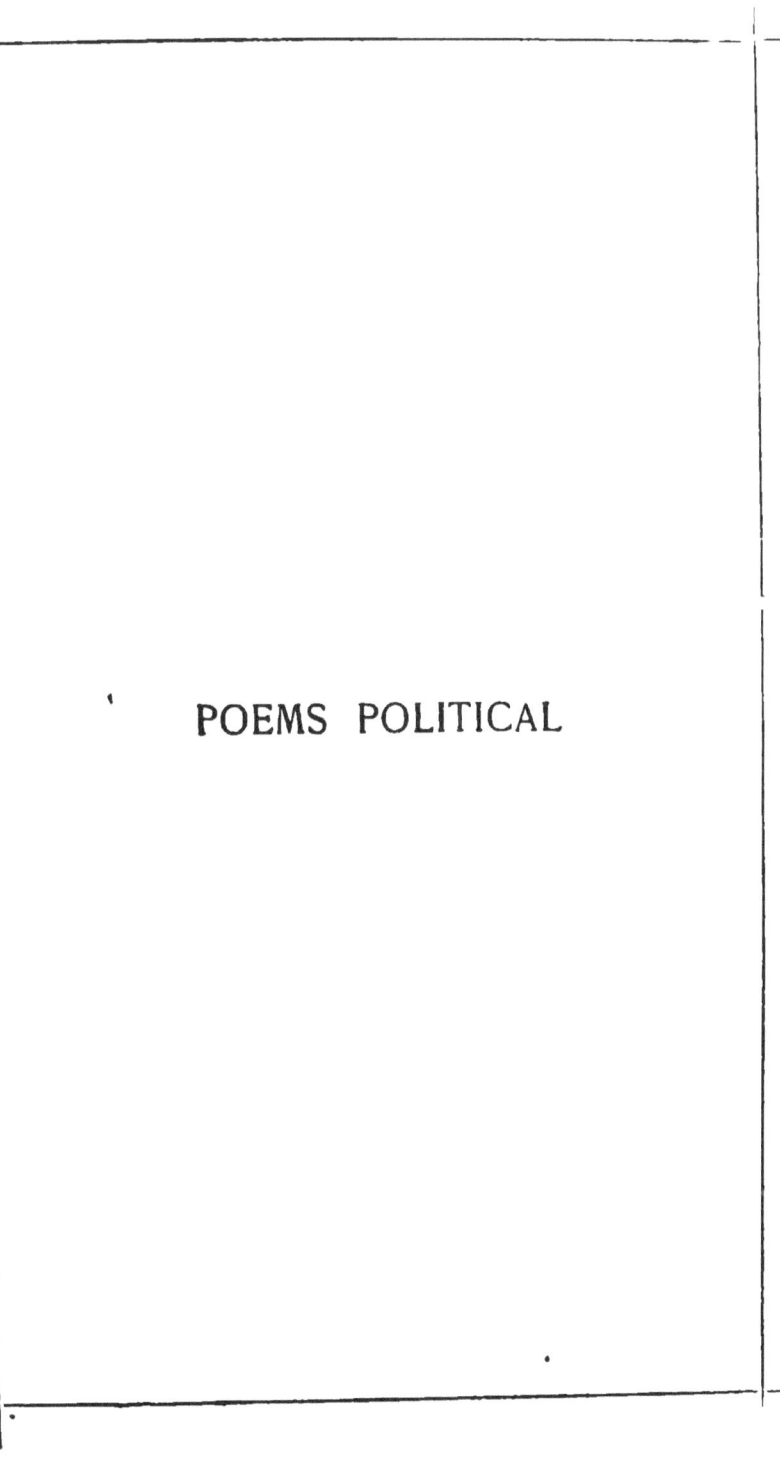

POEMS POLITICAL

APOLOGIA

In presenting the following poems to the public, in permanent form, the publisher is acting in direct disregard of the wishes of Mr. Kernan, who is anxious to let roses bloom where death-bolts fell in years of yore; but it would be utterly impossible to comply with his wishes, and at the same time give a fully rounded conception of his character. The bitter partisan hatred that was unleashed against him while in the North, because of his pronounced Southern sentiment, became intensified when he removed to the South, and in the frenzy of an abnormally sensitive nature, he wrote what follows. The Mr. Kernan of to-day insists that the hates conceived of slavery are deader than the dead hatreds of Hannibal and his hosts. He holds that we have only a common country now, in which partisan strife is only necessary to keep the atmosphere pure, clear and healthful.

I

O, Southland! loveliest land beneath the bright,
blue-bending skies!
O, land most passionate this side the gates of
Paradise!
A sense of gladness unconfined was mine when
first I set
My foot upon thy flowery sod: it lingers with
me yet.
I love thy immemorial hills by human kind
untrod;
The rose-lights of their raptured heights
touched by the kiss of God;
The crash and wirble jubilant of cataracts that
leap
And flash and shimmer through the vines that
trail from steep to steep.
I love thy valley-lands: they hold a beauty never
sung,
As sweet, as pure, as undefiled as when the
world was young.
As then the ripe, wild roses trail their scarlet
mists of bloom,
And sparkle sun-lit lily-bells with amber hearts
illume;
As then the rivers roll and surge,—proud, passionate and free,
Through sweeps of glad savanna-lands to kiss
the golden sea.
I love thy wild and waving woods where in the
glooms of green
The miracle magnolia-flowers like fallen moons
are seen,

Where mock-birds twitter, pipe and trill
　through long, resplendent days,
Till leaf and flower seem to dance in rhythm
　with their lays!
Cradle of Jefferson, Calhoun, and Davis— knight-
　liest one!
Whose name, whose high, white name, will
　shine and circle with the sun
　Until humanity no more its *immortelles* will
　twine,
Nor offer up bright votive blood at Freedom's
　altar-shrine!
O, land of roses and romance! of sunshine and
　of song!
The Grand All-Hail Hereafter will avenge thy
　ruth and wrong;
We can hear its portents thundering and see
　its flaming sign
As pearls into a purer light a day that is divine.
Down, faint hearts! down, false souls! at least
　this hour is not for thee,
Nor this the place for recreants to crook the
　ready knee.
Avaunt! nor thus insult our Faith, our Memo-
　ries, our Dead:
Remember heroes trod the spot whereon this
　night we tread!

II

Comrades! on these hills historic where up-
　flamed the battle-fire,
　Where upclashed keen swords to heaven in
　the dead and ruined years,
A fierce, remorseless canticle rings leaping
　from my lyre,
　A strain that echoes hate with hate, and an-
　swers sneers with sneers.

III

Out yonder sleep our sainted dead,—they died
  for you and me,
Out yonder, underneath the bright crown-
  jewels of the sky:
They fought because they loved our land; they
  fell to make us free;
They hold in heaven this night the truths
  divine that never die.

IV

The same grand Truths that glorified our war-
  flag when unfurled
They bore it on from height to height against
  our ancient foe,
What time their valor vivified, throughout the
  blue-ringed world,
Afresh the awful host of men by tyrants trampled low—

V

The Truths our Sires with b_...e-fires baptized
  in years of yore,
When they rebelled against the Wrong high-
  throned beyond the sea,
When they with bare, uplifted blades upon
  their altars swore,
By Father, Son and Holy Ghost this goodly
  land to free.

VI

That oath was kept, and Liberty walked smil-
  ing through our land
Sun-crowned, and blossoms fair upflowered
  where'er her footsteps fell;

Our peoplehood marched forward by a common
    feeling clanned
To the sweet, world-shaking music of the
    Independence Bell.

VII

But a doom runs through the ages; it was
    never known to fail,
In all the long-drawn cycles since our uni-
    verse began,
That plotters shall conspire, and with brand
    and ball assail
The liberties that beautify and bless their
    fellow-man.

VIII

In peril were our liberties—clanged high the
    tocsin peal—
The star and flower of Chivalry uprose to
    face the foe —
To face a countless foe that came to slaughter
    and to steal,
And with the battle-torch to lay our dear,
    old roof-trees low.

IX

Our warriors were fired by all the Lord holds
    leal,
By all that makes life beautiful, by all that
    makes men blessed,
By that duty the divinest, to uphold the com-
    mon weal,
And sacrifice the heart's red blood for broth-
    erhood oppressed.

X

In the white, shining track of Lee—the Rupert
    of his race—

They followed with unflagging feet, prepared
    to dree and die,
Through crash of shells, and storms of flame
    that smote them in the face,
While high their glorious Rebel yell rang
    grandly up the sky:

XI

While high through blinding cannon smoke
    the Southern Cross upflung
Its blazing folds, more terrible than battle-
    flag of Thor —
While roared red-throated rifles, and the sabers
    slashed and swung
To the wild, magnetic music of the thunder-
    drums of War.

XII

But there befell a tristful day: the Southern
    Cross went down
Before the Hessian hirelings from every shore
    and sea,—
The Hessian hirelings who fight for any flag
    or crown,
And trample in the very dust the White
    Rose of the Free.

XIII

Then came our cruel Iliad of wraths and
    wrongs; we saw
Our peoplehood deflowered of their birth-
    rights one by one,
What time the vile victor made his Christless
    creed our law,
And ruled our ruined Motherland with help
    of gyve and gun.

XIV

O, Stonewall, by the clear calm streams of
    Paradise this night!
  O, Barksdale, falling where the flood of con-
  flict reddest rolled!
O, Morgan, leading meteor-like thy cavalry in
    fight!
  O, Southern slain, or high or low, within
  the Gates of Gold!—

Now that our rights are repossessed, now that
    the foe has fled
  Beyond our borders, with the curse of crime
  upon his name —
Answer! Shall we still bend the knee, and
    shall we bow the head
  Unto his crimeful code, and thus forever
  seal our shame?

And from the Citadels of Christ—serene, and
    fair, and bright,
Their souls, communing with our souls, thus
    speak to us this night:

  By our Cause all grand and glorious,—
  Cause that yet will be victorious,—
By our banner, consecrated with the chrism of
    blood and tears, -
  Never!—Let the traitor perish
  Who would counsel ye to cherish
The black heresies we battled through the long
    and lurid years.

  It is not for ye to falter,
  It is not for ye to palter,
In this Crisis—for thy mission is the mightiest
    of time:

It is thine to lead a legion
Out of every realm and region
In the glorious march sunward to the Golden
    Heights sublime.

Rings the trump!—the drum is beating—
No retracting!—no retreating!—
Ye must tread the straight, white pathway that
    thy pure, proud martyrs trod,—
Teaching thus unto the foeman,
That ye truckle unto no man,
That thy birthland knows no master, save the
    one Great Master—God!

Up! and from thy statutes sever,
With a firm, swift hand forever,
All the laws antagonistic to thine august laws
    of old!
Strike for State-Rights! this thy mission,
Till it finds a full fruition —
Let the blessing of the ballot by Caucasians be
    controlled.

Up! rebuild thy ruined altars
That were shattered by assaulters,
And beside them swear thy children the same
    oath their fathers swore.
Thus the olden, golden glory,
Flashing through and through our story,
Like the splendor of a sunburst will illume
    Southland once more.

NO COMPROMISE

Shall we turn traitors, and forgive the Yankee
    hoodlum-horde
Who tramped through sunny Southland with
    the fagot and the sword?
No, never, by the God on high! until avenged
    shall be
Five hundred thousand Guards in Gray, who
    fell to make us free.'
Deep down within the heart of each white
    master of the South,
Though seldom written with the pen, or told
    by word of mouth,
There burns a purpose fierce and high, that
    yet will do and dare,
And when that coming hour chimes, let Yan-
    kee-land beware.

When foreigners invade her soil, our freedom
    we'll proclaim,
And smite her down into the depths of suffer-
    ing and shame;
Her fields shall be made desolate, her vengeful
    sons shall die:
Her cities, fired by our hands, paint hell upon
    the sky.
We bide our time, and He who waits in the
    translucent spheres
Will lead us to a sweet revenge in the on-thun-
    dering years;
The Stars and Bars will flash again within the
    Southern sky,
And then it shall be tooth for tooth—it shall
    be eye for eye!

THE SOUTHERN SLAIN

In their shrouds—the Stars and Bars—
Sleep to-night the Southern Slain,
Free from Midgard's mocking wars,
Fleeting joy and bitter pain.
Burning suns and languid moons
In their glory come and go—
Blooms the beauty of the Junes,
Sifts the sad December snow;
But beneath the Southern Cross
Still the wan, waste years wear by,
Bringing neither love nor loss,
Bridal-kiss nor burial cry—
Strewing only on each shrine
Ghost of lily, wraith of palm,
Where our martyrs—thine and mine—
Sleep in everlasting calm.
Mailèd hand and crownèd head
Rule their wrecked and ruined land:
Masters are the slaves—instead
Slaves the masters of her strand,
And the Hun-like victors hold
Orgies in her antique halls—
Brims the wine in cups of gold:
Full the festal-music falls—
Rounds the dance and rings the dice
In the silver lamp-light sheen,
While the victims of their vice,
Houseless, in her streets are seen.
In her capitols she hears
Vassal-voices where, sublime,
Thrilled the tones of Cavaliers
In the old, historic time.

But, save here and there, her sons
    Royal characters retain,
As when guardians of her guns
    On the blood-red battle-plain.
Still, in the sepulchral track
    Which their fainting footsteps trod,
Some have faithlessly turned back
    On their Goal and on their God;
Trailed the dear flag in the dust,
    Closer bound each brother's chain,
Call it "Treason," now, the Trust
    Left them by the Southern Slain.
But the glory and the gold
    Flung them by their foes shall be
Ashes, like the fable told
    Of the Apples of the Sea;
And their traitor-hearts shall turn
    Each into an adder's nest,
Till our planet pale shall spurn
    Them the rapture of its rest.
But beyond the Bifrost-pass
    Are the Southern Slain to-night.
In Valhalla's Courts of Glass,
    By palm-bordered waves of light,
Free from clash of clanging spears,
    Frost and fire of changing time,
Where the Valkyr's love endears
    Odin's perfect, perfect clime;
And their mausoleums tell
    Through their marble lips with pride,
How our heroes fought and fell;
    How our heroes dreed and died;
How they marched to martyr-graves
    Through funereal forests old,
By the sweep of isle-starred waves,
    Over mountain. fen and wold;
How they spread their silent camps

In the murky twilight mist,
Where distilled the dews and damps,
Where the hidden vipers hissed,
Where the Spanish-mosses swayed
In the spectral, moon-lit air,
Till a shroud their shadows made
For each fated sleeper there;
How like pillared cloud by day,
And like columned fire by night,
Still her banner showed the way,
Leading on from height to height,
Till the crisis came, and then
Was that flag of freedom furled,
And the throned and sceptered men,
Told a conquest to the world!
But, like Hannibal of old,
Every Southern youth will swear
At her altars hate untold
For the foes who fester there;
And that oath will sound our shame
Over field and over flood,
Till it flower into flame—
Till it blossom into blood!

WE NEVER WILL SUBMIT TO KINGS

Shall tan-yard tippler from the West
Assume the crown that Cæsar wore,
And place a new, imperial crest
Upon the flag our fathers bore?
Speak! shall he wrest from you and me
The liberty that is our boast?
Nay! nay!—By all the Powers that be—

By Father, Son and Holy Ghost,
By the pure, patriot blood that streamed
In '76 on plains and heights,
By the proud, patriot swords that gleamed
In all our grand, triumphant fights,
We swear to keep our powder dry,
Our rifles close at hand, until
He, in his wickedness, defy
The mandate of the public will,
When this shall be our battle-cry:
"KILL!"

Aye, kill the tyrant, and thus save
Full many a life, full many a home,—
Just as the Brutus, high and brave,
In the old, matchless days of Rome,
Killed Cæsar in his triumph-hour,
To wrest the sod from slavery,
And bade the bright, consummate flower
Of Freedom bloom from sea to sea!
Then let the Bloody Boor take heed,
Nor trifle with forbidden things,
For we, the People, have decreed
WE NEVER WILL SUBMIT TO KINGS.
We swear to keep our powder dry,
Our rifles close at hand, until
He in his wickedness defy
The mandate of the public will,
When this shall be our battle-cry:
"KILL!"

OUR CAUSE

"Hosanna! Hosanna!" we said,
"For the wealth of fruit and flowers,
For the beautiful presence of Peace
    That walks this inheritance wide!
The dream of the Plato dead
    Has come unto us and to ours,
And here is the sweet surcease
    And the white millennial tide!"

But a terrible doom leaps forth
    From the firm, invisible mouth,
    And, lo! for the earth is shaken,
        And horror is everywhere;
The Vandals rush from the North,
    The Chivalry rise in the South,
    And the sounds of their strife awaken
        The blue abysses of air.

One army showeth in splendor,
    Over many a moving gun,
    A blazing banner where beameth
        This prophecy unto man:
The South will never surrender
The Freedom the Fathers won—
    And ever this signal streameth
        All vividly in their van.

And what was the oath the others
    Sware slowly with bated breath,
    Under the skies blue-bending—
        What was the oath they swore?
Death to their bold, bright brothers,
    Ruin and shame and death,

265

And a whisperless hate unending
   Till all of the years be o'er.
We know how the oath was kept—
   With saber and chain and brand;
How it fires the felon-blood
   In the Puritan land away;
They have not slumbered or slept,
   But steadily, hand-in-hand,
      Through fire and yet through flood
      They have hounded us day by day.

     *   *   *   *   *

Could the lips of our pale dead part,
   And things all righteous reveal,
      This is the gospel of gold
         Their tongues would utter to-day:
Let the proud, pure Cavalier heart
   Its vow and its vengeance seal—
      Let a victory yet be told
         For the fallen Guards in Gray;—

For the old Confederate bands
   Who follow the waving plume,
      And the worn, gray uniform
         Of their Captain everywhere,
And who fell at length on the sands
   Of the Wilderness when the doom
      Of the last wild battle-storm
         Had smitten them with despair;—

For the young Confederate braves
   Who went in their manly might
      From the moss-draped manors old
         On the green hillsides away
And who fell by the far-off waves
   Where the blue seas blossom in white,
      Over glittering sands of gold,
         In the heart of a doomful day.

*   *   *   *   *

Go, then, to their burial-places,
  When the crimson and creamy blooms
    Are thridding the greenest grasses,
    Are twining the dim, old stones,
And think of their proud, still faces,
  In the depths of the desolate tombs,
    And say over them thy masses,
    And vent over them thy moans.

And swear by the blood of thy brothers
  Who fell on the battle-plain
    Swear by their graves all glorious,
    By the prayers thy sisters prayed,
Swear by the tears of thy mothers,
  By our passion and our pain,
    Forever, until victorious,
    For our Cause to stand arrayed.

AN ANONYMOUS ASSAILANT

I'd rather be the sneak that scrawls
His blackguard jingle on the walls,
Than skulk behind a stolen name,
And then, with dastard pen, defame,
In venomous and vulgar song,
A man who never did me wrong.
His the assassin's craven heart
Who thus directs the secret dart;
No earthly sin that you could name
Would flush his brow with honest shame;
No earthly vice he would not share
If he could find a pleasure there;

No crime that hell itself could bring
Would prove repugnant to this **THING.**

Of all created brutes, I know
None half so beastly and so low;
And apt that such a one should write
Weak rhodomontade to incite
The populace against my name,
Because my thoughts I dare proclaim.
May all my foes forever be
Such loathsome leper-hounds as he;
For me one service can they do—
But ONE—if to their natures true—
That service is to hate me well,
With all the burning hate of hell.

PECKSNIFFIAN POLITICIAN

1880

Stands he there upon the forum, and with
    thunder-tongue he cries.
"Will you vote for this hell-leper? will you
    thus forget his lies—
Lies his festered lips have sworn to by our
    Father in the skies?

"Will you thus forgive, O, people! one you
    trusted, and whose trust
He was bribed into betraying? Will you thus
    forgive his lust
For the lucre that hath led him to uphold a
    thing unjust?"

And the rabble roars in answer. "No! No! No!"
in accents high,
"Down to dust with this hell-spider! He hath
sworn unto a lie;
And we want no man to serve us whose sup-
port a bribe can buy."

1881

Shines the sun upon the White House on In-
auguration morn;
Up the stairs with step majestic stalks the man
they called foresworn,
And whose honesty, they howled, had by money
been o'erborne.

And he takes the oath of office. But a mad-
man sends a ball
Hissing through his very vitals. Then unto his
princely pall,
With a wreath of rose and lily comes his foeman first of all.

"O, my people!" speaks this foeman through
his crocodilean tears,
"Our beloved Chief hath fallen; he who leaves
no living peers;
He whose name will ring forever down the
thunder-march of years!

"He was spotless: search his record—and its
white, resplendent leaf
Is unsullied by an error, O, my brave and
blameless Chief!"
Then upspeaks a clear truth-teller, and in
language bold and brief,

Says: "Hold! Hold! I heard you howl just
one little year ago,

That this dead man was a liar, and that you
    could prove it so;
Was a thief, and you could prove it; now, sir,
    I would like to know

"Whether in your secret bosom you believe in
    what you say;
Were you lying *then*, or are you lying in your
    heart *to-day?*"
But the hypocrite goes slinking from his ques-
    tioner away.

O, this world! this world! It holdeth hordes of
    men who mete to you
Never once the even measure that is honestly
    your due,
And they trample on and over all who dare
    indeed be true.

They will hound you down and hiss you with
    a tiger-hate, but lo!
Scale unto a height of splendor that they may
    not hope to know,
And thenceforth they are your spaniels—abject,
    groveling and low.

FINIS

www.ingramcontent.com/pod-product-compliance
Lightning Source LLC
Chambersburg PA
CBHW020347030726
47496CB00007B/2031